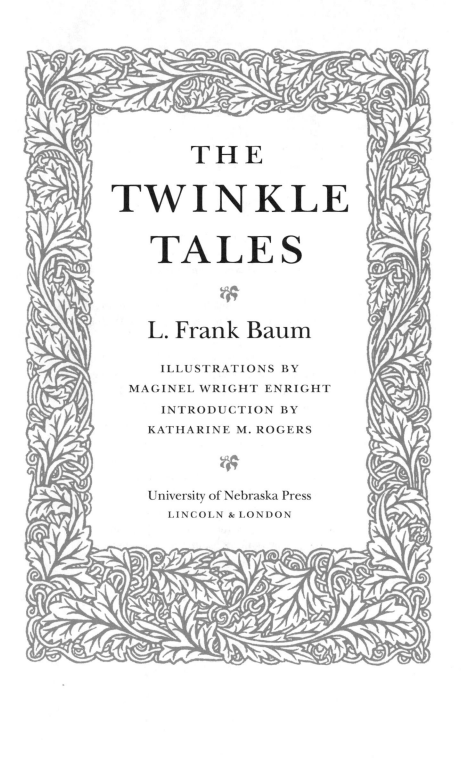

THE
TWINKLE
TALES

L. Frank Baum

ILLUSTRATIONS BY
MAGINEL WRIGHT ENRIGHT
INTRODUCTION BY
KATHARINE M. ROGERS

University of Nebraska Press
LINCOLN & LONDON

Library of Congress
Cataloging-in-Publication Data
Baum, L. Frank (Lyman Frank), 1856–1919
[Twinkle and Chubbins]
The Twinkle tales / L. Frank Baum ; illustrations by
Maginel Wright Enright ; introduction by Katharine M. Rogers.
p. cm.
New edition of two works previously published separately:
Twinkle and Chubbins, Kinderhook, Ill. : International
Wizard of Oz Club, 1987 ; and Policeman Bluejay, Delmar, N.Y. :
Scholar's Facsimiles & Reprints, 1981.
Summary : In Edgeley, South Dakota, two children,
Twinkle and Chubbins, explore the natural world and observe
as Policeman Bluejay enforces the laws of the birds
in an orderly forest world threatened only
by the wanton destructiveness of man.
ISBN 0-8032-6242-6 (pbk. : alk. paper)
[1. Birds – Fiction.   2. Nature – Fiction.   3. Fantasy.]
I. Barney, Maginel Wright, 1877– ill.   II. Baum, L. Frank
(Lyman Frank), 1856–1919 Policeman Bluejay.   III. Title.
PZ7.B327TW 2005
[Fic] – dc22   2005000871

Set in ITC New Baskerville by Kim Essman.
Designed by A. Shahan.
Printed by Thomson-Shore, Inc.

Contents

Illustrations

Twinkle's Enchantment

Sugar-Loaf Mountain

Policeman Bluejay

Introduction

Katharine M. Rogers

On October 6, 1905, L. Frank Baum signed a contract with his publisher, Reilly & Britton, to deliver by November 15 six children's stories, "written by him under the pen name of 'Laura Bancroft' or some female appellation of equally dignified comprehensiveness." In the same contract Baum promised to deliver two novels for teenage girls, also authored under the names of "mythological females"; a boys' adventure tale written under the pseudonym Captain Fitzgerald; and a novel for adults to be published under the name Schuyler Staunton. Both the number of books and the number of pen names were typical for Baum at the height of his career; he published an incredible six books in 1906 — those mentioned as well as *John Dough and the Cherub*, a fantasy for older children that appeared under his own name. Every year Baum would write at least one book in a series for teenage girls, one in a series for teenage boys, and one of the fantasies that he considered his real creative work.

Baum was forty-nine in 1905 and had at last become a successful writer. He had started out as an actor, then managed the family business in lubricating oil, run a fancy-goods store and edited a small-town newspaper in South Dakota, traveled around the Midwest selling china, and edited a trade journal for window decorators. Finally, he collaborated with the illustrator W. W. Denslow on two best-selling books: the now-forgotten *Father Goose* (1899), a collection of trifling verses, and *The Wonderful Wizard of Oz* (1900). By 1905 Baum had also published *The Marvelous Land of Oz* (1904) with Reilly & Britton, but he had not yet decided to focus on Oz and was still experimenting with various fairy countries.

Baum used his two and a half years' experience on the dry, treeless Dakota prairie in *The Wizard of Oz*, where, transposed to the similar terrain of Kansas, it provides an effectively contrasting starting point for Dorothy's wonderful adventures in Oz. He used the Dakota prairie as the actual setting of the Twinkle tales as well.[1] He and his wife, Maud, had lived quite comfortably in the small city of Aberdeen, but Maud's sister Julia Carpenter had been miserable on an isolated Dakota homestead and was not much happier when she moved into the tiny town of Edgeley. The Baums and the Carpenters maintained close contact after the Baums moved to Chicago and then to California; and Maud, the mother of four boys, was especially attached to Julia's daughter, Magdalena, who was a bright, outspoken child. Magdalena was the model for Twinkle and probably for Dorothy as well.

Baum acknowledged that he wrote the Twinkle tales "to earn some extra money," and by publishing them and *Policeman Bluejay* under the pseudonym Laura Bancroft he indicated that he took less pride in these writings than in the works that appeared under his own name.[2] Nevertheless, the tales, like almost all of his works for children, reveal flashes of the creative imagination and unconventional thinking that distinguish the Oz books as well as the realistic detail necessary to anchor the fantasy.

"Prairie-Dog Town" introduces Twinkle and her best friend, Chubbins, the son of the "tired-faced" local schoolteacher. The story is set in Edgeley, South Dakota, where the Carpenters lived. The school picnic must be held in the only bit of shade that can be found outside — under the bridge that crosses a muddy little stream "which they called a 'river,' but we would call only a brook." Twinkle and Chubbins go off exploring together and find a prairie-dog town. Imperceptibly, the two children move into a fantasy world in which they find themselves talking with the prairie dogs. In "Twinkle's Enchantment," Twinkle goes to a nearby gulch to pick blueberries for her papa's supper and realizes when a beetle warns her about crossing "the line of enchantment" that she must have crossed it already since she understood what the beetle was saying. In neither story, however, are there Oz-like wonders that seize the imagination. Beyond the line of enchantment Twinkle finds only a series of proverbial characters, such as the "Rolling Stone . . . that gathers no moss" and a weasel that goes "pop." "Prince Mud-Turtle" is a more traditional tale: Twinkle finds a beautifully colored mud turtle, learns that he is an enchanted prince, and helps him to regain his proper form.

In "Sugar-Loaf Mountain," Twinkle goes to visit Chubbins, who has moved to the Ozarks. They climb a nearby mountain, enter it through a trap door they discover, and ultimately arrive at a lovely underground city where the people are made of sugar. Regrettably, Baum distinguishes the upper classes of this make-believe world by describing them as made of pure white loaf sugar, while the lower classes are made of brown. Readers should realize that this casual, unconscious racism, also reflected in the title "Bandit Jim Crow," was virtually universal in Baum's day.

"Mister Woodchuck" is a more powerful tale because Baum uses it to make a point about human ethics. Twinkle's father sets a leg-hold trap to catch the woodchuck that is eating his red clover. When Twinkle falls asleep by the woodchuck hole she awakens to find herself reduced in size and forced to listen to

Mr. Woodchuck's point of view. She answers his denunciation of human beings who destroy woodchucks by protesting that a woodchuck that eats people's clover and vegetables has to be stopped. Mr. Woodchuck retorts that humans are selfish and cruel to torture "poor little animals that can't help themselves and have to eat what they can find, or starve." Simply killing them would not be so bad, he says: "Death doesn't last but an instant. But every minute of suffering [in a trap] seems to be an hour." Twinkle feels ashamed and that night persuades her father not to set any more traps: "Surely, papa, there's enough to eat in this big and beautiful world for all of God's creatures." Mr. Woodchuck's case against human self-centeredness and reproach for imposing the agony of the leg-hold trap takes this story well beyond the bland lessons of kindness to animals commonly preached in children's literature. Baum may have been moved to write about this topic because of his son Bob's accounts of hunting prairie dogs with his cousin Harry in Edgeley. The animals brought a one-cent bounty because they ate people's crops. If the boys had bullets, they shot the animals; otherwise they just smashed them.

Baum's moral is more conventional in "Bandit Jim Crow," the tale of a lawless, ungrateful crow that robs the nests of other birds. Eventually, the little birds, led by Policeman Blue Jay, mob the thankless crow and peck out his eyes. "Crows are tough, and this one was unlucky enough to remain alive," Baum commented. Because he is now afraid to leave his nest, he has to depend on the charity of the birds he has wronged to bring him food and water. "So Jim Crow, blind and helpless, sat in his nest day after day and week after week. . . . And I wonder what his thoughts were — don't you?" Despite this conclusion being unconventionally grim for children's fiction, Baum's child readers relished this unrelenting justice. "Bandit Jim Crow" proved to be the most popular of the tales.

Baum brought back Policeman Bluejay the following year, when "Laura Bancroft" published her best work, "Policeman Bluejay." This book (featured here as the seventh and concluding tale) is more substantial than the others: its plot is built on Baum's lifelong love and considerable knowledge of birds, and it introduces deeper and more unconventional moral criticism.[3] In the story, Twinkle and Chubbins get lost in the woods and close their eyes; they open them to see a hideous Tuxix, which turns them into skylarks when they refuse to do its bidding. Policeman Bluejay befriends the two child-larks and finds them an old nest to make their home. They meet Wisk the squirrel, tenant of the second-floor hollow in their tree, as well as other birds.

All the animals have stories of human cruelty. One tells how a hunter shot Susie Oriole's husband just when she had a nest of four eggs. Susie followed the man and found a room filled with stuffed birds, including her husband, as well as an egg collection, including the contents of her nest. A bobolink points out the irony: "How greatly those humans admire us birds. They make pictures of us, and love to keep us in cages so they can hear us sing, and they even wear us in their bonnets after we are dead." Robin Redbreast adds that "mankind is the most destructive and bloodthirsty of all the brute creation," since they kill not only for food but for personal adornment and even for amusement. In contrast, kind Mrs. Hootaway, the owl who occupies the top hollow of the child-larks' tree, kills only her natural prey, behavior compatible with "the Great Law of the forest," namely Love. Even though animals such as owls must kill and eat others in order to live, they practice love and tenderness for their own kind and for their neighbors as well. In a time when feathers were regularly used to decorate women's hats, when scientists studied animals by killing them, when hunting was generally accepted as a wholesome, manly pursuit, when farmers had no qualms about eradicating any "vermin" that threatened their crops, when humans considered themselves perfectly justified in wiping out animals that interfered with them in any way, Baum's moral message is strikingly original.

The child-larks are rudely awakened the next morning by a loud bang, shouts, barks, and screams of pain. Hunters have shot Mrs. 'Possum, the occupant of the first-floor burrow, and their dogs are tearing her babies apart. They then shoot the owl, whose last words are "Remember that — all — is love." Finally, the squirrel pokes his head out and is shot on sight. After the slaughter in the tree, Policeman Bluejay takes the child-larks to the Land of Paradise in the center of the forest, which is, appropriately, populated exclusively by birds of paradise. This happy country is totally free from the dangers and suffering that dominate life on the outside. Policeman Bluejay must even leave his nightstick at home when he approaches the gate; the Guardian Bird of Paradise does not like "to see anything that looks like a weapon. In his country there are no such things as quarrels or fighting, or naughtiness of any sort; for as they have everything they want there is nothing to quarrel over or fight for." Only "one race" lives in Paradise, "every member of which is quite particular not to annoy his fellows in any way."

Paradise is indeed perfect, although its beauty is disturbingly artificial: it is bathed in rosy radiance rather than sunlight; its trees are gold with silver leaves. Hostile feelings do not exist there. The King Bird, who is even more magnificently plumed than his subjects, welcomes the child-larks graciously, but he immediately asks them to admire his beauty. In a sterile, metallic forest, the king and the other male birds dance while delighting in their reflections in the silver leaves. The brown females sit in the background admiring them and occasionally rush forward to smooth a disarranged feather.

This land without need, evil, or conflict is indeed a paradise in its sharp contrast to the stressful life of the forest. However, the fortunate situation of the Birds of Paradise does not warrant their unquestioning self-satisfaction, which is based simply on abstaining from wrongdoing in the absence of temptation: everything they need for a comfortable life is constantly provided, and conflict cannot arise in a society that has bound itself to bland conformity. As the owl points out: "[They] are not obliged to take life in order to live themselves; so they call us savage and fierce. But I believe our natures are as kindly as those of the Birds of Paradise." They have not sinned, but in fact they have done no good deeds either; it is the scrappy Policeman Bluejay who helps the child-larks and the predatory Owl who maintains that all is love, even as she is being murdered.

By referring to a legend that man once lived in the Land of Paradise "but for some unknown crime was driven away," Baum clearly relates his paradise to the biblical Garden of Eden. Actually, he may have been hinting at an even more daring meaning, for "paradise" can mean Heaven as well as Eden. The King Bird of Paradise, who exists solely to be perfect and to be admired by his beautiful and sinless subjects, does bring to mind God surrounded by the heavenly hosts who constantly sing his praises. In either case, the Land of Paradise is not the ideal place of orthodox Christian doctrine. Baum's unfallen creatures are vacuous and complacent.

The undisturbed existence in Paradise contrasts strongly with the rich variety of Baum's Land of Oz, where every human, animal, and machine is accepted for what he or she is; where females are equal; where conflicts arise because people express their differing opinions; where adventures are possible because evil exists, though good always wins. For Baum, goodness is not a passive state but something achieved by effort and enterprise.

In *Policeman Bluejay* the Land of Paradise and the forest outside are both undesirable extremes; Baum implies that some evil and conflict are necessary if we are to live.

Baum did not subscribe to any of the traditional creeds, although he believed strongly in the reality of spirit. Like his mother-in-law, Matilda Gage, and other thoughtful contemporaries, he found a basis for his beliefs in theosophy, which claims to provide a rational basis for faith in a spiritual world by drawing on the essential truth that is found in all religions and in science as well. Theosophists believe that everyone has latent abilities that can be developed through resolution and effort so as to master oneself and the forces of nature. In the theosophist heaven, unlike the Land of Paradise, souls actively strive for the improvement of themselves and the world. Theosophy also emphasizes respect and concern for animals as beings not essentially different from humans — a constant theme in Laura Bancroft's stories.

The adventures described in the Twinkle tales and *Policeman Bluejay* were presented as dreams, presumably because they were supposed to have happened in America. However, in his preface to *Policeman Bluejay*, Baum dismissed this evasion by declaring that "in a fairy story it does not matter whether one is awake or not." Both magic adventures and dreams are real in the world of imagination, which has its own validity: Twinkle only dreamed her confrontation with Mister Woodchuck, but it gave her moral insight into our relationship with other animals. Baum may even have been implying that we can see truth better in dreams because they take us away from the everyday world and ordinary rational perceptions.

As he did in the Oz books, Baum introduced into the Laura Bancroft fairy stories witty philosophical speculations that engage adults. In the Twinkle tales, even more than in the Oz books, he introduced shocking bits of realism, such as the slaughter the child-larks witness in *Policeman Bluejay* and the fate of Bandit Jim Crow. Child readers could just pass over the philosophical aspects of the stories or interpret them literally, and they are strong enough to take — and hopefully profit from — the realism. Without leaving the level of fairy tale, the stories, especially *Policeman Bluejay,* move us to question accepted practices and beliefs, from our exploitation of animals to our assumptions about the nature of virtue, the necessity of evil, and the morality of pluming oneself on righteousness in the absence of temptation.

Feminism, an important theme throughout Baum's work, appears in these stories as well. Twinkle takes the lead more often than her friend Chubbins, and she is a typically enterprising and adventurous Baum girl. She is eager to cross the line that divides the common, real world from an enchanted country. She wants to visit the Gleaming Glade in the Land of Paradise because she is "determined to let nothing escape her that she could possibly see."

An important element in Baum's negative picture of Paradise is the subservient position of the females. They are not allowed to dance because they lack the brilliant plumage of the males. Twinkle thinks that "the brown birds with the soft gray breasts are just as pretty as the gaily clothed ones," however; and Chubbins disparages "the poor King," who doesn't have time to do anything but admire himself and look after his feathers.[4] Females are equal to males in the good societies Baum created in his works, subservient (or absent) in the bad ones.

Nearly forty thousand copies of the six individually published Twinkle tales sold in their first year. Reilly & Britton reissued them in a single volume, *Twinkle and Chubbins,* in 1911 and twice again as individual books after 1916. Although *Policeman Bluejay* was not successful by Baum standards — its first edition evidently did not go into a second printing — his publishers considered it worthwhile to reprint it under other guises. In 1911 it reappeared as *Babes in Birdland*, capitalizing on the popular *Babes in Toyland* (1903). In 1917 they reprinted it under Baum's name, although they vetoed his suggestion to enhance it further by calling it "An Oz Tale." In 1915 Baum told Reilly that he had always considered the Twinkle tales among his best stories, and he hoped they would some day be combined with *Policeman Bluejay* in a volume called "Baum's Wonder Book." Though Baum's preferred title was not selected for this publication, the present volume otherwise fulfills his wish.

Notes

1. Baum probably moved Dorothy from South Dakota to Kansas to spare the feelings of his wife's relatives, who still lived in South Dakota. In the Twinkle tales he depicts the plains less negatively: the region is odd rather than intolerably gray and dreary.

2. Michael Patrick Hearn, "When L. Frank Baum was 'Laura Bancroft,'" *American Book Collector* 8, no. 5 (May 1987): 11. Other information from Katharine M. Rogers, *L. Frank Baum: Creator of Oz* (New York: St. Martin's Press, 2002).

3. The female eagle is indeed bigger than the male, and male birds of paradise have fine plumage and gather in a group to dance and display themselves while the drab females watch. Perhaps, however, Baum did err in having the children transformed into larks, which are strictly grassland (not forest) birds.

4. Actually, as Baum may or may not have known, female birds of paradise watch the males dance not to admire but to judge them, to decide whom to choose as a mate.

Prairie-Dog Town

Chapter 1

The Picnic

On the great western prairies of Dakota is a little town called Edgeley, because it is on the edge of civilization — a very big word which means some folks have found a better way to live than other folks. The Edgeley people have a good way to live, for there are almost seventeen wooden houses there, and among them is a school-house, a church, a store and a blacksmith-shop. If people walked out their front doors they were upon the little street; if they walked out the back doors they were on the broad prairies. That was why Twinkle, who was a farmer's little girl, lived so near the town that she could easily walk to school.

She was a pretty, rosy-cheeked little thing, with long, fluffy hair, and big round eyes that everybody smiled into when the saw them. It was hard to keep that fluffy hair from getting tangled; so mamma used to tie it in the back with a big, broad ribbon. And Twinkle wore calico slips for school days and gingham dresses when she wanted to "dress up" or look especially nice. And to keep the sun from spotting her face with freckles, she wore sunbonnets made of the same goods as her dresses.

Twinkle's best chum was a little boy called Chubbins, who was the only child of the tired-faced school-teacher. Chubbins was about as old as Twinkle; but he wasn't so tall and slender for his age as she was, being short and rather fat. The hair on his

Chubbins

little round head was cut close, and he usually wore a shirt-waist and "knickers," with a wide straw hat on the back of his head. Chubbins's face was very solemn. He never said many words when grown folks were around, but he could talk fast enough when he and Twinkle were playing together alone.

Well, one Saturday the school had a picnic, and Twinkle and Chubbins both went. On the Dakota prairies there are no shade-trees at all, and very little water except what they get by boring deep holes in the ground; so you may wonder where the people could possibly have a picnic. But about three miles from the town a little stream of water (which they called a "river," but we would call only a brook) ran slow and muddy across the prairie; and where the road crossed it a flat bridge had been built. If you climbed down the banks of the river you would find a nice shady place under the wooden bridge; and so here it was that the picnics were held.

All the village went to the picnic, and they started bright and early in the morning, with horses and farm-wagons, and baskets full of good things to eat, and soon arrived at the bridge.

There was room enough in its shade for all to be comfortable; so they unhitched the horses and carried the baskets to the river bank, and began to laugh and be as merry as they could.

Twinkle and Chubbins, however, didn't care much for the shade of the bridge. This was a strange place to them, so they decided to explore it and see if it was any different from any other part of the prairie. Without telling anybody where they were going, they took hold of hands and trotted across the bridge and away into the plains on the other side.

The ground here wasn't flat, but had long rolls to it, like big waves on the ocean, so that as soon as the little girl and boy had climbed over the top of the first wave, or hill, those by the river lost sight of them.

They saw nothing but grass in the first hollow, but there was another hill just beyond, so they kept going, and climbed over that too. And now they found, lying in the second hollow, one of the most curious sights that the western prairies afford.

"What is it?" asked Chubbins, wonderingly.

"Why, it's a Prairie-Dog Town," said Twinkle.

Chapter 2

Prairie-Dog Town

Lying in every direction, and quite filling the little hollow, were round mounds of earth, each one having a hole in the center. The mounds were about two feet high and as big around as a washtub, and the edges of the holes were pounded hard and smooth by the pattering feet of the little creatures that lived within.

"Isn't it funny!" said Chubbins, staring at the mounds.

"Awful," replied Twinkle, staring too. "Do you know, Chub, there are an'mals living in every single one of those holes?"

"What kind?" asked Chubbins.

"Well, they're something like squirrels, only they *aren't* squirrels," he explained. "They're prairie-dogs."

"Don't like dogs," said the boy, looking a bit uneasy.

"Oh, they're not dogs at all," said Twinkle; "they're soft and fluffy, and gentle."

"Do they bark?" he asked.

"Yes; but they don't bite."

"How d' you know, Twinkle?"

"Papa has told me about them, lots of times. He says they're so shy that they run into their holes when anybody's around; but if you keep quiet and watch, they'll stick their heads out in a few minutes."

"Let's watch," said Chubbins.

7

"All right," she agreed.

Very near to some of the mounds was a raised bank, covered with soft grass; so the children stole softly up to this bank and lay down upon it in such a way that their heads just stuck over the top of it, while their bodies were hidden from the eyes of any of the folks of Prairie-Dog Town.

"Are you comferble, Chub?" asked the little girl.

"Yes." "Then lie still and don't talk, and keep your eyes open, and perhaps the an'mals will stick their heads up."

"All right," says Chubbins.

So they kept quiet and waited, and it seemed a long time to both the boy and the girl before a soft, furry head popped out of a near-by hole, and two big, gentle brown eyes looked at them curiously.

Chapter 3

Mr. Bowko, the Mayor

"Dear me!" said the prairie-dog, speaking almost in a whisper; "here are some of those queer humans from the village."

"Let me see! Let me see!" cried two shrill little voices, and the wee heads of two small creatures popped out of the hole and fixed their bright eyes upon the heads of Twinkle and Chubbins.

"Go down at once!" said the mother prairie-dog. "Do you want to get hurt, you naughty little things."

"Oh, they won't get hurt," said another deeper voice, and the children turned their eyes toward a second mound, on top of which sat a plump prairie-dog whose reddish fur was tipped with white on the end of each hair. He seemed to be quite old, or at least well along in years, and he had a wise and thoughtful look on his face.

"They're humans," said the mother.

"True enough; but they're only human children, and wouldn't hurt your little ones for the world," the old one said.

"That's so!" called Twinkle. "All we want, is to get acquainted."

"Why, in that case," replied the old prairie-dog, "you are very welcome in our town, and we're glad to see you."

"Thank you," said Twinkle, gratefully. It didn't occur to her just then that it was wonderful to be talking to the little prairie-dogs just as if they were people. It seemed very natural they should speak with each other and be friendly.

As if attracted by the sound of voices, little heads began to pop out of the other mounds — one here and one there — until the town was alive with the pretty creatures, all squatting near the edges of their holes and eyeing Chubbins and Twinkle with grave and curious looks.

"Let me introduce myself," said the old one that had first proved friendly. "My name is Bowko, and I'm the Mayor and High Chief of Prairie-Dog Town."

"Don't you have a king?" asked Twinkle.

"Not in this town," he answered. "There seems to be no place for kings in this free United States. And a Mayor and High Chief is just as good as a king, any day."

"I think so, too," answered the girl.

"Better!" declared Chubbins.

The Mayor smiled, as if pleased.

"I see you've been properly brought up," he continued; "and now let me introduce to you some of my fellow-citizens. This," pointing with one little paw to the hole where the mother and her two children were sitting, "is Mrs. Puff-Pudgy and her family — Teenty and Weenty. Mr. Puff-Pudgy, I regret to say, was recently chased out of town for saying his prayers backwards."

"How could he?" asked Chubbins, much surprised.

"He was always contrary," answered the Mayor, with a sigh, "and wouldn't do things the same way that others did. His good wife, Mrs. Puff-Pudgy, had to scold him all day long; so we finally made him leave the town, and I don't know where he's gone to."

"Won't he be sorry not to have his little children any more?" asked Twinkle, regretfully.

"I suppose so; but if people are contrary, and won't behave, they must take the consequences. This is Mr. Chuckledorf," continued the Mayor, and a very fat prairie-dog bowed to them most politely; "and here is Mrs. Fuzcum; and Mrs. Chatterby; and Mr. Sneezeley, and Doctor Dosem."

All these folks bowed gravely and politely, and Chubbins and Twinkle bobbed their heads in return until their necks ached, for it seemed as if the Mayor would never get through introducing the hundreds of prairie-dogs that were squatting around.

"I'll never be able to tell one from the other," whispered the girl; " 'cause they all look exactly alike."

"Some of 'em's fatter," observed Chubbins; "but I don't know which."

Chapter 4

Presto Digi, the Magician

A nd now, if you like, we will be pleased to have you visit some of our houses," said Mr. Bowko, the Mayor, in a friendly tone.

"But we can't" exclaimed Twinkle. "We're too big," and she got up and sat down upon the bank, to show him how big she really was when compared with the prairie-dogs.

"Oh, that doesn't matter in the least," the Mayor replied. "I'll have Presto Digi, our magician, reduce you to our size."

"Can he?" asked Twinkle, doubtfully.

"Our magician can do anything," declared the Mayor. Then he sat up and put both his front paws to his mouth and made a curious sound that was something like a bark and something like a whistle, but not exactly like either one.

Then everybody waited in silence until a queer old prairie-dog slowly put his head out of a big mound near the center of the village.

"Good morning, Mr. Presto Digi," said the Mayor.

"Morning!" answered the magician, blinking his eyes as if he had just awakened from sleep.

Twinkle nearly laughed at this scrawny, skinny personage; but by good fortune, for she didn't wish to offend him, she kept her face straight and did not even smile.

"We have two guests here, this morning," continued the

Mayor, addressing the magician, "who are a little too large to get into our houses. So, as they are invited to stay to luncheon, it would please us all if you would kindly reduce them to fit our underground rooms."

"Is *that* all you want?" asked Mr. Presto Digi, bobbing his head at the children.

"It seems to me a great deal," answered Twinkle. "I'm afraid you never could do it."

"Wow!" said the magician, in a scornful voice that was almost a bark. "I can do that with one paw. Come here to me, and don't step on any of our mounds while you're so big and clumsy."

So Twinkle and Chubbins got up and walked slowly toward the magician, taking great care where they stepped. Teenty and Weenty were frightened, and ducked their heads with little squeals as the big children passed their mound; but they bobbed up again the next moment, being curious to see what would happen.

When the boy and girl stopped before Mr. Presto Digi's mound, he began waving one of his thin, scraggy paws and at the same time made a gurgling noise that was deep down in his throat. And his eyes rolled and twisted around in a very odd way.

Neither Twinkle nor Chubbins felt any effect from the magic, nor any different from ordinary; but they knew they were growing smaller, because their eyes were getting closer to the magician.

"Is that enough?" asked Mr. Presto, after a while.

"Just a little more, please," replied the Mayor; I don't want them to bump their heads against the doorways."

So the magician again waved his paw and chuckled and gurgled and blinked, until Twinkle suddenly found she had to look up at him as he squatted on his mound.

Mr. Presto Digi works magic

"Stop!" she screamed; "if you keep on, we won't be anything at all!"

"You're just about the right size," said the Mayor, looking them over with much pleasure, and when the girl turned around she found Mr. Bowko and Mrs. Puff-Pudgy standing beside her, and she could easily see that Chubbins was no bigger than they, and she was no bigger than Chubbins.

"Kindly follow me," said Mrs. Puff-Pudgy, "for my little darlings are anxious to make your acquaintance, and as I was the first to discover you, you are to be my guests first of all, and afterward go to the Mayor's to luncheon."

Chapter 5

The Home of the Puff-Pudgys

So Twinkle and Chubbins, still holding hands, trotted along to the Puff-Pudgy mound, and it was strange how rough the ground now seemed to their tiny feet. They climbed up the slope of the mound rather clumsily, and when they came to the hole it seemed to them as big as a well. Then they saw that it wasn't a deep hole, but a sort of tunnel leading down hill into the mound, and Twinkle knew if they were careful they were not likely to slip or tumble down.

Mrs. Puff-Pudgy popped into the hole like a flash, for she was used to it, and waited just below the opening to guide them. So, Twinkle slipped down to the floor of the tunnel and Chubbins followed close after her, and then they began to go downward.

"It's a little dark right here," said Mrs. Puff-Pudgy; but I've ordered the maid to light the candles for you, so you'll see well enough when you're in the rooms."

"Thank you," said Twinkle, walking along the hall and feeling her way by keeping her hand upon the smooth sides of the passage. "I hope you won't go to any trouble, or put on airs, just because we've come to visit you."

"If I do," replied Mrs. Puff-Pudgy, "it's because I know the right way to treat company. We've always belonged to the 'four hundred,' you know. Some folks never know what to do, or how to do it, but that isn't the way with the Puff-Pudgys. Hi! you, Teenty and Weenty — get out of here and behave yourselves! You'll soon have a good look at our visitors."

And now they came into a room so comfortable and even splendid that Twinkle's eyes opened wide with amazement.

It was big, and of a round shape, and on the walls were painted very handsome portraits of different prairie-dogs of the Puff-Pudgy family. The furniture was made of white clay, baked hard in the sun and decorated with paints made from blue clay and red clay and yellow clay. This gave it a gorgeous appearance. There was a round table in the middle of the room, and several comfortable chairs and sofas. Around the walls were little brackets with candles in them, lighting the place very pleasantly.

"Sit down, please," said Mrs. Puff-Pudgy. "You'll want to rest a minute before I show you around."

So Twinkle and Chubbins sat upon the pretty clay chairs, and Teenty and Weenty sat opposite them and stared with their mischievous round eyes as hard as they could.

"What nice furniture," exclaimed the girl.

"Yes," replied Mrs. Puff-Pudgy, looking up at the picture of a sad-faced prairie-dog; "Mr. Puff-Pudgy made it all himself. He was very handy at such things. It's a shame he turned out so obstinate."

"Did he build the house too?"

"Why, he dug it out, if that's what you mean. But I advised him how to do it, so I deserve some credit for it myself. Next to the Mayor's, it's the best house in town, which accounts for our high social standing. Weenty! take your paw out of your mouth. You're biting your claws again."

"I'm not!" said Weenty.

"And now," continued Mrs. Puff-Pudgy, "if you are rested, I'll show you through the rest of our house."

So, they got up and followed her, and she led the children through an archway into the dining-room. Here was a cupboard full of the cunningest little dishes Twinkle had ever seen. They were all made of clay, baked hard in the sun, and were of graceful shapes, and nearly as smooth and perfect as our own dishes.

Chapter 6

Teenty and Weenty

All around the sides of the dining-room were pockets, or bins, in the wall; and these were full of those things the prairie-dogs are most fond of eating. Clover-seeds filled one bin, and sweet roots another; dried mulberry leaves — that must have come from a long distance — were in another bin, and even kernels of yellow field corn were heaped in one place. The Puff-Pudgys were surely in no danger of starving for some time to come.

"Teenty! Put back that grain of wheat," commanded the mother, in a severe voice.

Instead of obeying, Teenty put the wheat in his mouth and ate it as quickly as possible.

"The little dears are *so* restless," Mrs. Puff-Pudgy said to Twinkle, "that it's hard to manage them."

"They don't behave," remarked Chubbins, staring hard at the children.

"No, they have a share of their father's obstinate nature," replied Mrs. Puff-Pudgy. "Excuse me a minute and I'll cuff them; it'll do them good."

But before their mother could reach them, the children found trouble of their own. Teenty sprang at Weenty and began to fight, because his brother had pinched him, and Weenty fought back with all his might and main. They scratched with their claws and bit with their teeth, and rolled over and over upon the floor, bumping into the wall and upsetting the chairs, and snarling and growling all the while like two puppies.

Mrs. Puff-Pudgy sat down and watched them, but did not interfere.

"Won't they hurt themselves?" asked Twinkle, anxiously.

"Perhaps so," said the mother; "but if they do, it will punish them for being so naughty. I always let them fight it out, because they are so sore for a day or two afterward that they have to keep quiet, and then I get a little rest."

Weenty set up a great howling, just then, and Teenty drew away from his defeated brother and looked at him closely. The fur on both of them was badly mussed up, and Weenty had a long scratch on his nose, that must have hurt him, or he wouldn't have howled so. Teenty's left eye was closed tight, but if it hurt him he bore the pain in silence.

Mrs. Puff-Pudgy now pushed them both into a little room and shut them up, saying they must stay there until bedtime; and then she led Twinkle and Chubbins into the kitchen and showed them a pool of clear water, in a big clay basin, that had been caught during the last rain and saved for drinking purposes. The children drank of it, and found it cool and refreshing.

Then they saw the bedrooms, and learned that the beds of prairie-dogs were nothing more than round hollows made in heaps of clay. These animals always curl themselves up when they sleep, and the round hollows just fitted their bodies; so, no doubt, they found them very comfortable.

There were several bedrooms, for the Puff-Pudgy house was really very large. It was also very cool and pleasant, being all underground and not a bit damp.

After they had admired everything in a way that made Mrs. Puff-Pudgy very proud and happy, their hostess took one of the lighted candles from a bracket and said she would now escort them to the house of the Honorable Mr. Bowko, the Mayor.

Chapter 7

The Mayor Gives a Luncheon

"Don't we have to go upstairs and out of doors?" asked Twinkle.

"Oh, no," replied the prairie-dog, "we have halls connecting all the different houses of importance. Just follow me, and you can't get lost."

They might easily have been lost without their guide, the little girl thought, after they had gone through several winding passages. They turned this way and that, in quite a bewildering manner, and there were so many underground tunnels going in every direction that it was a wonder Mrs. Puff-Pudgy knew which way to go.

"You ought to have sign-posts," said Chubbins, who had once been in a city.

"Why, as for that, every one in the town knows which way to go," answered their guide; "and it isn't often we have visitors. Last week a gray owl stopped with us for a couple of days, and we had a fine ball in her honor. But you are the first humans that have ever been entertained in our town, so it's quite an event with us." A few minutes later she said: "Here we are, at the Mayor's house," and as they passed under a broad archway she blew out her candle, because the Mayor's house was so brilliantly lighted.

"Welcome!" said Mr. Bowko, greeting the children with polite bows. "You are just in time, for luncheon is about ready and my guests are waiting for you."

He led them at once into a big dining-room that was so magnificently painted with colored clays that the walls were as bright as a June rainbow.

"How pretty!" cried Twinkle, clapping her hands together in delight.

"I'm glad you like it," said the Mayor, much pleased. "Some people, who are lacking in good taste, think it's a little overdone, but a Mayor's house should be gorgeous, I think, so as to be a credit to the community. My grandfather, who designed and painted this house, was a very fine artist. But luncheon is ready, so pray be seated."

They sat down on little clay chairs that were placed at the round table. The Mayor sat on one side of Twinkle and Mrs. Puff-Pudgy on the other, and Chubbins was between the skinny old magician and Mr. Sneezeley. Also, in other chairs sat Dr. Dosem, and Mrs. Chatterby, and Mrs. Fuzcum, and several others. It was a large company, indeed, which showed that the Mayor considered this a very important occasion.

They were waited upon by several sleek prairie-dog maids in white aprons and white caps, who looked neat and respectable, and were very graceful in their motions.

Neither Twinkle nor Chubbins was very hungry, but they were curious to know what kind of food the prairie-dogs ate, so they watched carefully when the different dishes were passed around. Only grains and vegetables were used, for prairie-dogs do not eat meat. There was a milk-weed soup at first; and then yellow corn, boiled and sliced thin. Afterward they had a salad of thistle leaves, and some bread made of barley. The dessert was a dish of the sweet, dark honey made by prairie-bees, and some cakes flavored with sweet and spicy roots that only prairie-dogs know how to find.

The children tasted of several dishes, just to show their politeness; but they couldn't eat much. Chubbins spent most of his time watching Mr. Presto Digi, who ate up everything that was near him and seemed to be as hungry after the luncheon as he had been before.

Mrs. Puff-Pudgy talked so much about the social standing and dignity of the Puff-Pudgys that she couldn't find time to eat much, although she asked for the recipe of the milk-weed soup. But most of the others present paid strict attention to the meal and ate with very good appetites.

Chapter 8

On Top of the Earth Again

Afterward they all went into the big drawing-room, where Mrs. Fuzcum sang a song for them in a very shrill voice, and Mr. Sneezeley and Mrs. Chatterby danced a graceful minuet that was much admired by all present.

"We ought to be going home," said Twinkle, after this entertainment was over. "I'm afraid our folks will worry about us."

"We regret to part with you," replied the Mayor; "but, if you really think you ought to go, we will not be so impolite as to urge you to stay."

"You'll find we have excellent manners," added Mrs. Puff-Pudgy.

"I want to get big again," said Chubbins.

"Very well; please step this way," said the Mayor.

So they all followed him through a long passage until they began to go upward, as if climbing a hill. And then a gleam of daylight showed just ahead of them, and a few more steps brought them to the hole in the middle of the mound.

The Mayor and Mrs. Puff-Pudgy jumped up first, and then they helped Twinkle and Chubbins to scramble out. The strong sunlight made them blink their eyes for a time, but when they were able to look around they found one or more heads of prairie-dogs sticking from every mound.

"Now, Mr. Presto Digi," said the Mayor, when all the party

"Do you think we've been asleep?"

were standing on the ground, "please enlarge our friends to their natural sizes again."

"That is very easy," said the magician, with a sigh. "I really wish, Mr. Mayor, that you would find something for me to do that is difficult."

"I will, some time," promised the Mayor. "Just now, this is all I can require of you."

So the magician waved his paw and gurgled, much in the same way he had done before, and Twinkle and Chubbins began to grow and swell out until they were as large as ever, and the prairie-dogs again seemed very small beside them.

"Good-bye," said the little girl, "and thank you all, very much, for your kindness to us."

"Good-bye!" answered a chorus of small voices, and then all the prairie-dogs popped into their holes and quickly disappeared.

Twinkle and Chubbins found they were sitting on the green bank again, at the edge of Prairie-Dog Town.

"Do you think we've been asleep, Chub?" asked the girl.

" 'Course not," replied Chubbins, with a big yawn. "It's easy 'nough to know that, Twink, 'cause I'm sleepy now!"

Bandit Jim Crow

Chapter 1

Jim Crow Becomes a Pet

One day, when Twinkle's father was in the corn-field, he shot his gun at a flock of crows that were busy digging up, with their long bills, the kernels of corn he had planted. But Twinkle's father didn't aim very straight, for the birds screamed at the bang of the gun and quickly flew away — all except one young crow that fluttered its wings, but couldn't rise into the air, and so began to run along the ground in an effort to escape.

The man chased the young crow, and caught it; and then he found that one of the little lead bullets had broken the right wing, although the bird seemed not to be hurt in any other way.

It struggled hard, and tried to peck the hands that held it; but it was too young to hurt any one, so Twinkle's father decided he would carry it home to his little girl.

"Here's a pet for you, Twinkle," he said, as he came into the house. "It can't fly, because its wing is broken; but don't let it get too near your eyes, or it may peck at them. It's very wild and fierce, you know."

Twinkle was delighted with her pet, and at once got her mother to bandage the broken wing, so that it would heal quickly.

The crow had jet black feathers, but there was a pretty purplish and violet gloss, or sheen, on its back and wings, and its eyes were bright and had a knowing look in them. They were hazel-brown in color, and the bird had a queer way of turning his head on one side to look at Twinkle with his right eye, and then twisting it to the other side that he might see her with his left eye. She often wondered if she looked the same to both eyes, or if each one made her seem different.

She named her pet "Jim Crow" because papa said that all crows were called Jim, although he never could find out the reason. But the name seemed to fit her pet as well as any, so Twinkle never bothered about the reason.

Having no cage to keep him in, and fearing he would run away, the girl tied a strong cord around one of Jim Crow's legs, and the other end of the cord she fastened to the round of a chair — or to the table-leg — when they were in the house. The crow would run all around, as far as the string would let him go; but he couldn't get away. And when they went out of doors Twinkle held the end of the cord in her hand, as one leads a dog, and Jim Crow would run along in front of her, and then stop and wait. And when she came near he'd run on again, screaming "Caw! Caw!" at the top of his shrill little voice.

He soon came to know he belonged to Twinkle, and would often lie in her lap or perch upon her shoulder. And whenever she entered the room where he was he would say, "Caw — caw!" to her, in pleading tones, until she picked him up or took some notice of him.

It was wonderful how quickly a bird that had always lived wild and free seemed to become tame and gentle. Twinkle's father said that was because he was so young, and because his broken wing kept him from flying in the air and rejoining his fellows. But Jim Crow wasn't as tame as he seemed, and he had a very wicked and ungrateful disposition, as you will presently learn.

For a few weeks, however, he was as nice a pet as any little girl could wish for. He got into mischief occasionally, and caused mamma some annoyance when he waded into a pan of milk or jumped upon the dinner table and ate up papa's pumpkin pie before Twinkle could stop him. But all pets are more or less trouble, at times, so Jim Crow escaped with a few severe scoldings from mamma, which never seemed to worry him in the least or make him a bit unhappy.

Chapter 2

Jim Crow Runs Away

A t last Jim got so tame that Twinkle took the cord off his leg and let him go free, wherever he pleased. So he wandered all over the house and out into the yard, where he chased the ducks and bothered the pigs and made himself generally disliked. He had a way of perching upon the back of old Tom, papa's favorite horse, and chattering away in Tom's ear until the horse plunged and pranced in his stall to get rid of his unwelcome visitor.

Twinkle always kept the bandage on the wounded wing, for she didn't know whether it was well yet, or not, and she thought it was better to be on the safe side. But the truth was, that Jim Crow's wing had healed long ago, and was now as strong as ever; and, as the weeks passed by, and he grew big and fat, a great longing came into his wild heart to fly again — far, far up into the air and away to the lands where there were forests of trees and brooks of running water.

He didn't ever expect to rejoin his family again. They were far enough away by this time. And he didn't care much to associate with other crows. All he wanted was to be free, and do exactly as he pleased, and not have some one cuffing him a dozen times a day because he was doing wrong.

So one morning, before Twinkle was up, or even awake, Jim Crow pecked at the bandage on his wing until he got the end

Jim gets rid of his bandage

unfastened, and then it wasn't long before the entire strip of cloth was loosened and fell to the ground.

Now Jim fluttered his feathers, and pruned them with his long bill where they had been pressed together, and presently he knew that the wing which had been injured was exactly as strong and well as the other one. He could fly away whenever he pleased.

The crow had been well fed by Twinkle and her mamma, and was in splendid health. But he was not at all grateful. With the knowledge of his freedom a fierce, cruel joy crept into his heart, and he resumed the wild nature that crows are born with and never lay aside as long as they live.

Having forgotten in an instant that he had ever been tame, and the pet of a gentle little girl, Jim Crow had no thought of saying good-bye to Twinkle. Instead, he decided he would do something that would make these foolish humans remember him for a long time. So he dashed into a group of young chickens that had only been hatched a day or two before, and killed seven of them with his strong, curved claws and his wicked black beak. When the mother hen flew at him he pecked at her eyes; and then, screaming a defiance to all the world, Jim Crow flew into the air and sailed away to a new life in another part of the world.

Chapter 3

Jim Crow Finds a New Home

I 'll not try to tell you of all the awful things this bad crow did during the next few days, on his long journey toward the South.

Twinkle almost cried when she found her pet gone; and she really did cry when she saw the poor murdered chickens. But mamma said she was very glad to have Jim Crow run away, and papa scowled angrily and declared he was sorry he had not killed the cruel bird when he shot at it in the corn-field.

In the mean time the runaway crow flew through the country, and when he was hungry he would stop at a farm-house and rob a hen's nest and eat the eggs. It was his knowledge of farm-houses that made him so bold; but the farmers shot at the thieving bird once or twice, and this frightened Jim Crow so badly that he decided to keep away from the farms and find a living in some less dangerous way.

And one day he came to a fine forest, where there were big and little trees of all kinds, with several streams of water running through the woods.

"Here," said Jim Crow, "I will make my home; for surely this is the finest place I am ever likely to find."

There were plenty of birds in this forest, for Jim could hear them singing and twittering everywhere among the trees; and their nests hung suspended from branches, or nestled in a fork made by two limbs, in almost every direction he might look. And the birds were of many kinds, too: robins, thrushes, bullfinches, mocking-birds, wrens, yellowtails and skylarks. Even tiny humming-birds fluttered around the wild flowers that grew in the glades; and in the waters of the brooks waded long-legged herons, while kingfishers sat upon overhanging branches and waited patiently to seize any careless fish that might swim too near them.

Jim Crow decided this must be a real paradise for birds, because it was far away from the houses of men. So he made up his mind to get acquainted with the inhabitants of the forest as soon as possible, and let them know who he was, and that he must be treated with proper respect.

In a big fir-tree, whose branches reached nearly to the ground, he saw a large gathering of the birds, who sat chattering and gossiping pleasantly together. So he flew down and joined them.

"Good morning, folks," he said; and his voice sounded to them like a harsh croak, because it had become much deeper in tone since he had grown to his full size.

The birds looked at him curiously, and one or two fluttered their wings in a timid and nervous way; but none of them, little or big, thought best to make any reply.

"Well," said Jim Crow, gruffly, "what's the matter with you fellows? Haven't you got tongues? You seemed to talk fast enough a minute ago."

"Excuse me," replied a bullfinch, in a dignified voice; "we haven't the honor of your acquaintance. You are a stranger."

"My name's Jim Crow," he answered, "and I won't be a stranger long, because I'm going to live here."

They all looked grave at this speech, and a little thrush hopped from one branch to another, and remarked:

"We haven't any crows here at all. If you want to find your own folks you must go to some other place."

"What do I care about my own folks?" asked Jim, with a laugh that made the little thrush shudder. "I prefer to live alone."

"Haven't you a mate?" asked a robin, speaking in a very polite tone.

"No; and I don't want any," said Jim Crow. "I'm going to live all by myself. There's plenty of room in this forest, I guess."

"Certainly," replied the bullfinch. "There is plenty of room for you here if you behave yourself and obey the laws."

"Who's going to make me?" he asked, angrily.

"Any decent person, even if he's a crow, is bound to respect the law," answered the bullfinch, calmly.

Jim Crow was a little ashamed, for he didn't wish to acknowledge he wasn't decent. So he said:

"What are your laws?"

"The same as those in all other forests. You must respect the nests and the property of all other birds, and not interfere with them when they're hunting for food. And you must warn your fellow-birds whenever there is danger, and assist them to protect their young from prowling beasts. If you obey these laws, and do not steal from or interfere with your neighbors, you have a right to a nest in our forest."

"To be quite frank with you, though," said the robin, "we prefer your room to your company."

"I'm going to stay," said the crow. "I guess I'm as good as the rest of you; so you fellows just mind your own business and I'll mind mine."

With these words he left them, and when he had mounted to a position above the trees he saw that one tall, slim pine was higher than all the rest, and that at its very top was a big deserted nest.

Chapter 4

Jim Crow Becomes a Robber

I t looked like a crow's nest to Jim, so he flew toward the pine tree and lit upon a branch close by. One glance told him that at some time it really must have been the home of birds of his kind, who for some reason had abandoned it long ago. The nest was large and bulky, being made of strong sticks woven together with fine roots and grasses. It was rough outside, but smooth inside, and when Jim Crow had kicked out the dead leaves and twigs that had fallen into it, he decided it was nearly as good as new, and plenty good enough for a solitary crow like him to live in. So with his bill he made a mark on the nest, that every bird might know it belonged to him, and felt that at last he had found a home.

During the next few days he made several attempts to get acquainted with the other birds, but they were cold and distant, though very polite to him; and none of them seemed to care for his society.

No bird ever came near his nest, but he often flew down to the lower trees and perched upon one or another of them, so gradually the birds of the forest got used to seeing him around, and paid very little attention to his actions.

One day Mrs. Wren missed two brown eggs from her nest, and her little heart was nearly broken with grief. It took the mocking bird and the bullfinch a whole afternoon to comfort her, while Mr. Wren hopped around in nearly as much distress as his wife. No animals had been seen in the forest who would do this evil thing, so no one could imagine who the thief might be.

Such an outrage was almost unknown in this pleasant forest, and it made all the birds nervous and fearful. A few days later a still greater horror came upon them, for the helpless young children of Mrs. Linnet were seized one morning from their nest, while their parents were absent in search of food, and were carried away bodily. Mr. Linnet declared that on his way back to his nest he had seen a big black monster leaving it, but had been too frightened to notice just what the creature looked like. But the lark, who had been up very early that morning, stated that he had seen no one near that part of the forest except Jim Crow, who had flown swiftly to his nest in the tall pine-tree.

This was enough to make all the birds look upon Jim Crow with grave suspicion, and Robin Redbreast called a secret meeting of all the birds to discuss the question and decide what must be done to preserve their nests from the robber. Jim Crow was so much bigger and fiercer than any of the others that none dared accuse him openly or venture to quarrel with him; but they had a good friend living not far away who was not afraid of Jim Crow or any one else, so they finally decided to send for him and ask his assistance.

The starling undertook to be the messenger, and as soon as the meeting was over he flew away upon his errand.

"What were all you folks talking about?" asked the crow, flying down and alighting upon a limb near to those who had not yet left the place of meeting.

"We were talking about you," said the thrush, boldly; "and you wouldn't care at all to know what we said, Mister Jim Crow."

Jim looked a trifle guilty and ashamed at hearing this, but

knowing they were all afraid of him he burst out into a rude laugh.

"Caw! caw! caw!" he chuckled hoarsely; "what do I care what you say about me? But don't you get saucy, my pretty thrush, or your friends will miss you some fine morning, and never see you again."

This awful threat made them all silent, for they remembered the fate of poor Mrs. Linnet's children, and very few of the birds now had any doubt but that Jim Crow knew more about the death of those helpless little ones than he cared to tell.

Finding they would not talk with him, the crow flew back to his tree, where he sat sullenly perched upon a branch near his nest. And they were very glad to get rid of him so easily.

Chapter 5

Jim Crow Meets Policeman Blue Jay

Next morning Jim Crow woke up hungry, and as he sat lazily in his big nest, he remembered that he had seen four pretty brown eggs, speckled with white, in the nest of the oriole that lived at the edge of the forest.

"Those eggs will taste very good for breakfast," he thought. "I'll go at once and get them; and if old Mammy Oriole makes a fuss, I'll eat her, too."

He hopped out of his nest and on to a branch, and the first thing his sharp eye saw was a big and strange bird sitting upon the tree just opposite him and looking steadily in his direction.

Never having lived among other birds until now, the crow did not know what kind of bird this was, but as he faced the new-comer he had a sort of shiver in his heart that warned him to beware an enemy. Indeed, it was none other than the Bluc Jay that had appeared so suddenly, and he had arrived that morning because the starling had told him of the thefts that had taken place, and the Blue Jay is well known as the policeman of the forest and a terror to all evil-doers.

In size he was nearly as big as Jim Crow himself, and he had a large crest of feathers on the top of his head that made him look even more fierce — especially when he ruffled them up. His body was purplish blue color on the back and purplish gray below, and there was a collar of black feathers running all around his neck. But his wings and tail were a beautiful rich blue, as delightful in color as the sky on a fine May morning; so in personal appearance Policeman Blue Jay was much handsomer than Jim Crow. But it was the sharp, stout beak that most alarmed the crow, and had Jim been wiser he would have known that before him was the most deadly foe of his race, and that the greatest pleasure a Blue Jay finds in life is to fight with and punish a crow.

But Jim was not very wise; and so he imagined, after his first terror had passed away, that he could bully this bird as he had the others, and make it fear him.

"Well, what are you doing here?" he called out, in his crossest voice, for he was anxious to get away and rob the oriole's nest.

The Blue Jay gave a scornful, chattering laugh as he answered:

"That's none of your business, Jim Crow."

"Take care!" warned the crow; "you'll be sorry if you don't treat me with proper respect."

The Blue Jay winked solemnly, in a way that would have been very comical to any observer other than the angry crow.

"Don't hurt me — please don't!" he said, fluttering on the branch as if greatly frightened. "My mother would feel dreadful bad if anything happened to me."

"Well, then, behave yourself," returned the crow, strutting proudly along a limb and flopping his broad wings in an impressive manner. For he was foolish enough to think he had made the other afraid.

But no sooner had he taken flight and soared into the air than the Blue Jay darted at him like an arrow from a bow, and before Jim Crow could turn to defend himself the bill of his enemy struck him full in the breast. Then, with a shriek of shrill laughter, the policeman darted away and disappeared in the forest, leaving the crow to whirl around in the air once or twice and then sink slowly down, with some of his own torn feathers floating near him as witnesses to his defeat.

The attack had dazed and astonished him beyond measure; but he found he was not much hurt, after all. Crows are tougher than most birds. Jim managed to reach one of the brooks, where he bathed his breast in the cool water, and soon he felt much refreshed and more like his old self again.

But he decided not to go to the oriole's nest that morning, but to search for grubs and beetles amongst the mosses beneath the oak-trees.

Chapter 6

Jim Crow Fools the Policeman

From that time on Policeman Blue Jay made his home in the forest, keeping a sharp eye upon the actions of Jim Crow. And one day he flew away to the southward and returned with Mrs. Blue Jay, who was even more beautiful than her mate. Together they built a fine nest in a tree that stood near to the crow's tall pine, and soon after they had settled down to housekeeping Mrs. Blue Jay began to lay eggs of a pretty brown color mottled with darker brown specks.

Had Jim Crow known what was best for him he would have flown away from this forest and found himself a new home. Within a short flight were many bits of woodland where a crow might get a good living and not be bothered by blue jays. But Jim was obstinate and foolish, and had made up his mind that he never would again be happy until he had been revenged upon his enemy.

He dared no longer rob the nests so boldly as he had before, so he became sly and cunning. He soon found out that the Blue Jay could not fly as high as he could, nor as fast; so, if he kept a sharp lookout for the approach of his foe, he had no trouble in escaping. But if he went near to the nests of the smaller birds, there was the blue policeman standing guard, and ready and anxious to fight at a moment's notice. It was really no place for a robber at all, unless the robber was clever.

One day Jim Crow discovered a chalk-pit among the rocks at the north of the forest, just beyond the edge of trees. The chalk was soft and in some places crumbled to a fine powder, so that when he had rolled himself for a few minutes in the dust all his feathers became as white as snow. This fact gave to Jim Crow a bright idea. No longer black, but white as a dove, he flew away to the forest and passed right by Policeman Blue Jay, who only noticed that a big white bird had flown amongst the trees, and did not suspect it was the thieving crow in a clever disguise.

Jim found a robin's nest that was not protected, both the robin and his wife being away in search of food. So he ate up the eggs and kicked the nest to pieces and then flew away again, passing the Blue Jay a second time all unnoticed.

When he reached a brook he washed all the chalk away from his feathers and then returned to his nest as black as ever.

All the birds were angry and dismayed when the found what had happened, but none could imagine who had robbed the robins. Mrs. Robin, who was not easily discouraged, built another nest and laid more eggs in it; but the next day a second nest in the forest was robbed, and then another and another, until the birds complained that Policeman Blue Jay did not protect them at all.

"I can't understand it in the least," said the policeman, "for I have watched carefully, and I know Jim Crow has never dared to come near to your trees."

"Then some one else is the robber," declared the thrush fussily.

"The only stranger I have noticed around here is a big white bird," replied the Blue Jay, "and white birds never rob nests or eat eggs, as you all know very well."

So they were no nearer the truth than before, and the thefts continued; for each day Jim Crow would make himself white in the chalk-pit, fly into the forest and destroy the precious eggs of some innocent little bird, and afterward wash himself in some far-away brook, and return to his nest chuckling with glee to think he had fooled the Blue Jay so nicely.

But the Blue Jay, although stupid and unsuspecting at first, presently began to get a little wisdom. He remembered that all this trouble had commenced when the strange white bird first arrived in the forest; and although it was doubtless true that white birds never eat eggs and have honest reputations, he decided to watch this stranger and make sure that it was innocent of the frightful crimes that had so aroused the dwellers in the forest.

Chapter 7

Jim Crow Is Punished

S o one day Policeman Blue Jay hid himself in some thick bushes until he saw the big white bird fly by, and then he followed quietly after it, flitting from tree to tree and keeping out of sight as much as possible, until at last he saw the white bird alight near a bullfinch's nest and eat up all the eggs it contained.

Then, ruffling his crest angrily, Policeman Blue Jay flew to attack the big white robber, and was astonished to find he could not catch it. For the white bird flew higher into the air than he could, and also flew much faster, so that it soon escaped and passed out of sight.

"It must be a white crow," thought the Blue Jay; "for only a crow can beat me at flying, and some of that race are said to be white, although I have never seen one."

So he called together all the birds, and told them what he had seen, and they all agreed to hide themselves the next day and lie in wait for the thief.

By this time Jim Crow thought himself perfectly safe, and success had made him as bold as he was wicked. Therefore he suspected nothing when, after rolling himself in the chalk, he flew down the next day into the forest to feast upon birds' eggs. He soon came to a pretty nest, and was just about to rob it, when a chorus of shrill cries arose on every side of him and hundreds

The birds of the forest

of birds — so many that they quite filled the air — flew straight at the white one, pecking him with their bills and striking him with their wings; for anger had made even the most timid of the little birds fierce, and there were so many of them that they gave each other courage.

Jim Crow tried to escape, but whichever way he might fly his foes clustered all around him, getting in his way so that he could not use his big wings properly. And all the time they were pecking at him and fighting him as hard as they could. Also, the chalk was brushed from his feathers, by degrees, and soon the birds were able to recognize their old enemy the crow, and then, indeed, they became more furious than ever.

Policeman Blue Jay was especially angry at the deception practiced upon him, and if he could have got at the crow just then he would have killed it instantly. But the little birds were all in his way, so he was forced to hold aloof.

Filled with terror and smarting with pain, Jim Crow had only one thought: to get in the shelter of his nest in the pine-tree. In some way he managed to do this, and to sink exhausted into the hollow of his nest. But many of his enemies followed him, and although the thick feathers of his back and wings protected his body, Jim's head and eyes were at the mercy of the sharp bills of the vengeful birds.

When at last they left him, thinking he had been sufficiently punished, Jim Crow was as nearly dead as a bird could be. But crows are tough, and this one was unlucky enough to remain alive. For when his wounds had healed he had become totally blind, and day after day he sat in his nest, helpless and alone, and dared not leave it.

The birds bear water to Jim

Chapter 8

Jim Crow Has Time to Repent His Sins

"Where are you going, my dear?" asked the Blue Jay of his wife.

"I'm going to carry some grubs to Jim Crow," she answered. "I'll be back in a minute."

"Jim Crow is a robber and a murderer!" said the policeman, harshly.

"I know," she replied, in a sweet voice; "but he is blind."

"Well, fly along," said her husband; "but hurry back again."

And the robin-redbreast and his wife filled a cup-shaped flower with water from the brook, and then carried it in their bills to the pine-tree, without spilling a drop.

"Where are you going?" asked the oriole, as they passed.

"We're just taking some water to Jim Crow," replied Mrs. Robin.

"He's a thief and a scoundrel!" cried the oriole, indignantly.

"That is true," said Mrs. Robin, in a soft, pitiful voice; "but he is blind."

"Let me help you," exclaimed the oriole. "I'll carry this side of the cup, so it can't tip."

So Jim Crow, blind and helpless, sat in his nest day after day and week after week, while the little birds he had so cruelly wronged brought him food and water and cared for him as generously as they could.

And I wonder what his thoughts were — don't you?

Mr. Woodchuck

Chapter 1

The Trap

"There's a woodchuck over on the side hill that is eating my red clover," said Twinkle's father, who was a farmer.

"Why don't you set a trap for it?" asked Twinkle's mother.

"I believe I will," answered the man.

So, when the midday dinner was over, the farmer went to the barn and got a steel trap, and carried it over to the clover-field on the hillside.

Twinkle wanted very much to go with him, but she had to help mamma wash the dishes and put them away, and then brush up the dining-room and put it in order. But when the work was done, and she had all the rest of the afternoon to herself, she decided to go over to the woodchuck's hole and see how papa had set the trap, and also discover if the woodchuck had yet been caught.

So the little girl took her blue-and-white sun-bonnet, and climbed over the garden fence and ran across the corn-field and through the rye until she came to the red-clover patch on the hill.

She knew perfectly well where the woodchuck's hole was, for she had looked at it curiously many times; so she approached it carefully and found the trap set just in front of the hole. If the woodchuck stepped on it, when he came out, it would grab his

Twinkle waits for the woodchuck

leg and hold him fast; and there was a chain fastened to the trap, and also to a stout post driven into the ground, so that when the woodchuck was caught he couldn't run away with the trap.

But although the day was bright and sunshiny, and just the kind of day woodchucks like, the clover-eater had not yet walked out of his hole to get caught in the trap.

So Twinkle lay down in the clover-field, half hidden by a small bank in front of the woodchuck's hole, and began to watch for the little animal to come out. Her eyes could see right into the hole, which seemed to slant upward into the hill instead of downward; but of course she couldn't see very far in, because the hole wasn't straight, and grew black a little way from the opening.

It was somewhat wearisome, waiting and watching so long, and the warm sun and the soft chirp of the crickets that hopped through the clover made Twinkle drowsy. She didn't intend to go to sleep, because then she might miss the woodchuck; but there was no harm in closing her eyes just one little minute; so she allowed the long lashes to droop over her pretty pink cheeks — just because they felt so heavy, and there was no way to prop them up.

Then, with a start, she opened her eyes again, and saw the trap and the woodchuck hole just as they were before. Not quite, though, come to look carefully. The hole seemed to be bigger than at first; yes, strange as it might seem, the hole was growing bigger every minute! She watched it with much surprise, and then looked at the trap, which remained the same size it had always been. And when she turned her eyes upon the hole once more it had not only become very big and high, but a stone arch appeared over it, and a fine, polished front door now shut it off from the outside world. She could even read a name upon the silver door-plate, and the name was this:

MISTER WOODCHUCK

Chapter 2

Mr. Woodchuck Captures a Girl

"Well, I declare!" whispered Twinkle to herself; "how could all that have happened?"

On each side of the door was a little green bench, big enough for two to sit upon, and between the benches was a doorstep of white marble, with a mat lying on it. On one side Twinkle saw an electric door-bell.

While she gazed at this astonishing sight a sound of rapid footsteps was heard, and a large Jack-Rabbit, almost as big as herself, and dressed in a messenger-boy's uniform, ran up to the woodchuck's front door and rang the bell.

Almost at once the door opened inward, and a curious personage stepped out.

Twinkle saw at a glance that it was the woodchuck himself, — but what a big and queer woodchuck it was!

He wore a swallow-tailed coat, with a waistcoat of white satin and fancy knee-breeches, and upon his feet were shoes with silver buckles. On his head was perched a tall silk hat that made him look just as high as Twinkle's father, and in one paw he held a gold-headed cane. Also he wore big spectacles over his eyes, which made him look more dignified than any other woodchuck Twinkle had ever seen.

When this person opened the door and saw the Jack-Rabbit messenger-boy, he cried out:

"Well, what do you mean by ringing my bell so violently? I suppose you're half an hour late, and trying to make me think you're in a hurry."

The Jack-Rabbit took a telegram from its pocket and handed it to the woodchuck without a word in reply. At once the woodchuck tore open the envelope and read the telegram carefully.

"Thank you. There's no answer," he said; and in an instant the Jack-Rabbit had whisked away and was gone.

"Well, well," said the woodchuck, as if to himself, "the foolish farmer has set a trap for me, it seems, and my friends have sent a telegram to warn me. Let's see — where is the thing?"

He soon discovered the trap, and seizing hold of the chain he pulled the peg out of the ground and threw the whole thing far away into the field.

"I must give that farmer a sound scolding," he muttered, "for he's becoming so impudent lately that soon he will think he owns the whole country."

But now his eyes fell upon Twinkle, who lay in the clover staring up at him; and the woodchuck gave a laugh and grabbed her fast by one arm.

"Oh ho!" he exclaimed; "you're spying upon me, are you?"

"I'm just waiting to see you get caught in the trap," said the girl, standing up because the big creature pulled upon her arm. She wasn't much frightened, strange to say, because this woodchuck had a good-humored way about him that gave her confidence.

"You would have to wait a long time for that," he said, with a laugh that was a sort of low chuckle. "Instead of seeing me caught, you've got caught yourself. That's turning the tables, sure enough; isn't it?"

"I suppose it is," said Twinkle, regretfully. "Am I a prisoner?"

"You might call it that; and then, again, you mightn't," answered the woodchuck. "To tell you the truth, I hardly know

Mr. Woodchuck discovers Twinkle

what to do with you. But come inside, and we'll talk it over. We musn't be seen out here in the fields."

Still holding fast to her arm, the woodchuck led her through the door, which he carefully closed and locked. Then they passed through a kind of hallway, into which opened several handsomely furnished rooms, and out again into a beautiful garden at the back, all filled with flowers and brightly colored plants, and with a pretty fountain playing in the middle. A high stone wall was built around the garden, shutting it off from all the rest of the world.

The woodchuck led his prisoner to a bench beside the fountain, and told her to sit down and make herself comfortable.

Chapter 3

Mr. Woodchuck Scolds Twinkle

T winkle was much pleased with her surroundings, and soon discovered several gold-fishes swimming in the water at the foot of the fountain.

"Well, how does it strike you?" asked the woodchuck, strutting up and down the gravel walk before her and swinging his gold-headed cane rather gracefully.

"It seems like a dream," said Twinkle.

"To be sure," he answered, nodding.

"You'd no business to fall asleep in the clover."

"Did I?" she asked, rather startled at the suggestion.

"It stands to reason you did," he replied. "You don't for a moment think this is real, do you?"

"It *seems* real," she answered. "Aren't you the woodchuck?"

"*Mister* Woodchuck, if you please. Address me properly, young lady, or you'll make me angry."

"Well, then, aren't you Mister Woodchuck?"

"At present I am; but when you wake up, I won't be," he said.

"Then you think I'm dreaming?"

"You must figure that out for yourself," said Mister Wood-chuck.

"What do you suppose made me dream?"

"I don't know."

"Do you think it's something I've eaten?" she asked anxiously.

"I hardly think so. This isn't any nightmare, you know, because there's nothing at all horrible about it — so far. You've probably been reading some of those creepy, sensational storybooks."

"I haven't read a book in a long time," said Twinkle.

"Dreams," remarked Mister Woodchuck, thoughtfully, "are not always to be accounted for. But this conversation is all wrong. When one is dreaming one doesn't talk about it, or even know it's a dream. So let's speak of something else."

"It's very pleasant in this garden," said Twinkle. "I don't mind being here a bit."

"But you can't stay here," replied Mister Woodchuck, "and you ought to be very uncomfortable in my presence. You see, you're one of the deadliest enemies of my race. All you human beings live for or think of is how to torture and destroy woodchucks."

"Oh, no!" she answered. "We have many more important things than that to think of. But when a woodchuck gets eating our clover and the vegetables, and spoils a lot, we just have to do something to stop it. That's why my papa set the trap."

"You're selfish," said Mister Woodchuck, "and you're cruel to poor little animals that can't help themselves, and have to eat what they can find, or starve. There's enough for all of us growing in the broad fields."

Twinkle felt a little ashamed.

"We have to sell the clover and the vegetables to earn our living," she explained; "and if the animals eat them up we can't sell them."

"We don't eat enough to rob you," said the woodchuck, "and the land belonged to the wild creatures long before you people came here and began to farm. And really, there is no reason why you should be so cruel. It hurts dreadfully to be caught in a trap, and an animal captured in that way sometimes has to

65

suffer for many hours before the man comes to kill it. We don't mind the killing so much. Death doesn't last but an instant. But every minute of suffering seems to be an hour."

"That's true," said Twinkle, feeling sorry and repentant. "I'll ask papa never to set another trap."

"That will be some help," returned Mister Woodchuck, more cheerfully, "and I hope you'll not forget the promise when you wake up. But that isn't enough to settle the account for all our past sufferings, I assure you; so I am trying to think of a suitable way to punish you for the past wickedness of your father, and of all other men that have set traps."

"Why, if you feel that way," said the little girl, "you're just as bad as we are!"

"How's that?" asked Mister Woodchuck, pausing in his walk to look at her.

"It's as naughty to want revenge as it is to be selfish and cruel," she said.

"I believe you are right about that," answered the animal, taking off his silk hat and rubbing the fur smooth with his elbow. "But woodchucks are not perfect, any more than men are, so you'll have to take us as you find us. And now I'll call my family, and exhibit you to them. The children, especially, will enjoy seeing the wild human girl I've had the luck to capture."

"Wild!" she cried, indignantly.

"If you're not wild now, you will be before you wake up," he said.

Chapter 4

Mrs. Woodchuck and Her Family

But Mister Woodchuck had no need to call his family, for just as he spoke a chatter of voices was heard and Mrs. Woodchuck came walking down a path of the garden with several young woodchucks following after her.

The lady animal was very fussily dressed, with puffs and ruffles and laces all over her silk gown, and perched upon her head was a broad white hat with long ostrich plumes. She was exceedingly fat, even for a woodchuck, and her head fitted close to her body, without any neck whatever to separate them. Although it was shady in the garden, she held a lace parasol over her head, and her walk was so mincing and airy that Twinkle almost laughed in her face.

The young woodchucks were of several sizes and kinds. One little woodchuck girl rolled before her a doll's baby-cab, in which lay a woodchuck doll made of cloth, in quite a perfect imitation of a real woodchuck. It was stuffed with something soft to make it round and fat, and its eyes were two glass beads sewn upon the face. A big boy woodchuck wore knickerbockers and a Tam o'Shanter cap and rolled a hoop; and there were several smaller boy and girl woodchucks, dressed quite as absurdly, who followed after their mother in a long train.

"My dear," said Mister Woodchuck to his wife, "here is a human creature that I captured just outside our front door."

"Huh!" sneered the lady woodchuck, looking at Twinkle in a very haughty way; "why will you bring such an animal into our garden, Leander? It makes me shiver just to look at the horrid thing!"

"Oh, mommer!" yelled one of the children, "see how skinny the beast is!"

"Hasn't any hair on its face at all," said another, "or on its paws!"

"And no sign of a tail!" cried the little woodchuck girl with the doll.

"Yes, it's a very strange and remarkable creature," said the mother. "Don't touch it, my precious darlings. It might bite."

"You needn't worry," said Twinkle, rather provoked at these speeches. "I wouldn't bite a dirty, greasy woodchuck on any account!"

"Whoo! did you hear what she called us, mommer? She says we're greasy and dirty!" shouted the children, and some of them grabbed pebbles from the path in their paws, as if to throw them at Twinkle.

"Tut, tut! don't be cruel," said Mister Woodchuck. "Remember the poor creature is a prisoner, and isn't used to good society; and besides that, she's dreaming."

"Really?" exclaimed Mrs. Woodchuck, looking at the girl curiously.

"To be sure," he answered. "Otherwise she wouldn't see us dressed in such fancy clothes, nor would we be bigger than she is. The whole thing is unnatural, my dear, as you must admit."

"But *we're* not dreaming; are we, Daddy?" anxiously asked the boy with the hoop.

"Certainly not," Mister Woodchuck answered; "so this is a fine opportunity for you to study one of those human animals who have always been our worst enemies. You will notice they are very curiously made. Aside from their lack of hair in any place except the top of the head, their paws are formed in a strange manner. Those long slits in them make what are called fingers, and their claws are flat and dull — not at all sharp and strong like ours."

"I think the beast is ugly," said Mrs. Woodchuck. "It would give me the shivers to touch its skinny flesh."

"I'm glad of that," said Twinkle, indignantly. "You wouldn't have *all* the shivers, I can tell you! And you're a disagreeable, ign'rant creature! If you had any manners at all, you'd treat strangers more politely."

"Just listen to the thing!" said Mrs. Woodchuck, in a horrified tone. "Isn't it wild, though!"

Chapter 5

Mr. Woodchuck Argues the Question

"Really," Mister Woodchuck said to his wife, "you should be more considerate of the little human's feelings. She is quite intelligent and tame, for one of her kind, and has a tender heart, I am sure."

"I don't see anything intelligent about her," said the girl woodchuck.

"I guess I've been to school as much as you have," said Twinkle.

"School! Why, what's that?"

"Don't you know what school is?" cried Twinkle, much amused.

"We don't have school here," said Mister Woodchuck, as if proud of the fact.

"Don't you know any geography?" asked the child.

"We haven't any use for it," said Mister Woodchuck; "for we never get far from home, and don't care a rap what state bounds Florida on the south. We don't travel much, and studying geography would be time wasted."

"But don't you study arithmetic?" she asked; "don't you know how to do sums?"

"Why should we?" he returned. "The thing that bothers you humans most, and that's money, is not used by us woodchucks. So we don't need to figure and do sums."

"I don't see how you get along without money," said Twinkle, wonderingly. "You must have to buy all your fine clothes."

"You know very well that woodchucks don't wear clothes, under ordinary circumstances," Mister Woodchuck replied. "It's only because you are dreaming that you see us dressed in this way."

"Perhaps that's true," said Twinkle. "But don't talk to me about not being intelligent, or not knowing things. If you haven't any schools it's certain I know more than your whole family put together!"

"About some things, perhaps," acknowledged Mister Woodchuck. "But tell me: do you know which kind of red clover is the best to eat?"

"No," she said.

"Or how to dig a hole in the ground to live in, with different rooms and passages, so that it slants up hill and the rain won't come in and drown you?"

"No," said Twinkle.

"And could you tell, on the second day of February (which is woodchuck day, you know), whether it's going to be warm weather, or cold, during the next six weeks?"

"I don't believe I could," replied the girl.

"Then," said Mister Woodchuck, "there are some things that we know that you don't; and although a woodchuck might not be of much account in one of your schoolrooms, you must forgive me for saying that I think you'd make a mighty poor woodchuck."

"I think so, too!" said Twinkle, laughing.

"And now, little human," he resumed, after looking at his watch, "it's nearly time for you to wake up; so if we intend to punish you for all the misery your people has inflicted on the woodchucks, we won't have a minute to spare."

"Don't be in a hurry," said Twinkle. "I can wait."

71

"She's trying to get out of it," exclaimed Mrs. Woodchuck, scornfully. "Don't you let her, Leander."

"Certainly not, my dear," he replied; "but I haven't decided how to punish her."

"Take her to Judge Stoneyheart," said Mrs. Woodchuck. "He will know what to do with her."

Chapter 6

Twinkle is Taken to the Judge

A t this the woodchuck children all hooted with joy, crying: "Take her, Daddy! Take her to old Stoneyheart! Oh, my! won't he give it to her, though!"

"Who is Judge Stoneyheart?" asked Twinkle, a little uneasily.

"A highly respected and aged woodchuck who is cousin to my wife's grandfather," was the reply. "We consider him the wisest and most intelligent of our race; but, while he is very just in all things, the judge never shows any mercy to evil-doers."

"I haven't done anything wrong," said the girl.

"But your father has, and much wrong is done us by the other farmers around here. They fight my people without mercy, and kill every woodchuck they can possibly catch."

Twinkle was silent, for she knew this to be true.

"For my part," continued Mister Woodchuck, "I'm very soft-hearted, and wouldn't even step on an ant if I could help it. Also I am sure you have a kind disposition. But you are a human, and I am a woodchuck; so I think I will take you to old Stoneyheart and let him decide your fate."

"Hooray!" yelled the young woodchucks, and away they ran through the paths of the garden, followed slowly by their fat mother, who held the lace parasol over her head as if she feared she would be sunstruck.

Twinkle was glad to see them go. She didn't care much for

the woodchuck children, they were so wild and ill-mannered, and their mother was even more disagreeable than they were. As for Mister Woodchuck, she did not object to him so much; in fact, she rather liked to talk to him, for his words were polite and his eyes pleasant and kindly.

"Now, my dear," he said, "as we are about to leave this garden, where you have been quite secure, I must try to prevent your running away when we are outside the wall. I hope it won't hurt your feelings to become a real prisoner for a few minutes."

Then Mister Woodchuck drew from his pocket a leather collar, very much like a dog-collar, Twinkle thought, and proceeded to buckle it around the girl's neck. To the collar was attached a fine chain about six feet long, and the other end of the chain Mister Woodchuck held in his hand.

"Now, then," said he, "please come along quietly, and don't make a fuss."

He led her to the end of the garden and opened a wooden gate in the wall, through which they passed. Outside the garden was nothing but hard, baked earth, without any grass or other green thing growing upon it, or any tree or shrub to shade it from the hot sun. And not far away stood a round mound, also of baked earth, which Twinkle at once decided to be a house, because it had a door and some windows in it.

There was no living thing in sight — not even a woodchuck — and Twinkle didn't care much for the baked-clay scenery.

Mister Woodchuck, holding fast to the chain, led his prisoner across the barren space to the round mound, where he paused to rap softly upon the door.

Chapter 7

Twinkle Is Condemned

"Come in!" called a voice.

Mister Woodchuck pushed open the door and entered, drawing Twinkle after him by the chain.

In the middle of the room sat a woodchuck whose hair was grizzled with old age. He wore big spectacles upon his nose, and a round knitted cap, with a tassel dangling from the top, upon his head. His only garment was an old and faded dressing-gown.

When they entered, the old woodchuck was busy playing a game with a number of baked-clay dominoes, which he shuffled and arranged upon a baked-mud table; nor did he look up for a long time, but continued to match the dominoes and to study their arrangement with intense interest.

Finally, however, he finished the game, and then he raised his head and looked sharply at his visitors.

"Good afternoon, Judge," said Mister Woodchuck, taking off his silk hat and bowing respectfully.

The judge did not answer him, but continued to stare at Twinkle.

"I have called to ask your advice," continued Mister Woodchuck. "By good chance I have been able to capture one of those fierce humans that are the greatest enemies of peaceful woodchucks."

The judge nodded his gray head wisely, but still answered nothing.

"But now that I've captured the creature, I don't know what to do with her," went on Mister Woodchuck; "although I believe, of course, she should be punished in some way, and made to feel as unhappy as her people have made us feel. Yet I realize that it's a dreadful thing to hurt any living creature, and as far as I'm concerned I'm quite willing to forgive her. With these words he wiped his face with a red silk handkerchief, as if really distressed.

"She's dreaming," said the judge, in a sharp, quick voice.

"Am I?" asked Twinkle.

"Of course. You were probably lying on the wrong side when you went to sleep."

"Oh!" she said. "I wondered what made it."

"Very disagreeable dream, isn't it?" continued the judge.

"Not so very," she answered. "It's interesting to see and hear woodchucks in their own homes, and Mister Woodchuck has shown me how cruel it is for us to set traps for you."

"Good!" said the judge. "But some dreams are easily forgotten, so I'll teach you a lesson you'll be likely to remember. You shall be caught in a trap yourself."

"Me!" cried Twinkle, in dismay.

"Yes, you. When you find how dreadfully it hurts you'll bear the traps in mind forever afterward. People don't remember dreams unless the dreams are unusually horrible. But I guess you'll remember this one."

He got up and opened a mud cupboard, from which he took a big steel trap. Twinkle could see that it was just like the trap papa had set to catch the woodchucks, only it seemed much bigger and stronger.

The judge got a mallet and with it pounded a stake into the mud floor. Then he fastened the chain of the trap to the stake,

The judge fetches a trap

and afterward opened the iron jaws of the cruel-looking thing and set them with a lever, so that the slightest touch would spring the trap and make the strong jaws snap together.

"Now, little girl," said he, "you must step in the trap and get caught."

"Why, it would break my leg!" cried Twinkle.

"Did your father care whether a woodchuck got its leg broken or not?" asked the judge.

"No," she answered, beginning to be greatly frightened.

"Step!" cried the judge, sternly.

"It will hurt awfully," said Mister Woodchuck; "but that can't be helped. Traps are cruel things, at the best."

Twinkle was not trembling with nervousness and fear.

"Step!" called the judge, again.

"Dear me!" said Mister Woodchuck, just then, as he looked earnestly into Twinkle's face, "I believe she's going to wake up!"

"That's too bad," said the judge.

"No, I'm glad of it," replied Mister Woodchuck.

And just then the girl gave a start and opened her eyes.

She was lying in the clover, and before her was the opening of the woodchuck's hole, with the trap still set before it.

Chapter 8

Twinkle Remembers

"Papa," said Twinkle, when supper was over and she was nestled snugly in his lap, "I wish you wouldn't set any more traps for the woodchucks."

"Why not, my darling?" he asked in surprise.

"They're cruel," she answered. "It must hurt the poor animals dreadfully to be caught in them."

"I suppose it does," said her father, thoughtfully. "But if I don't trap the woodchucks they eat our clover and vegetables."

"Never mind that," said Twinkle, earnestly. "Let's divide with them. God made the woodchucks, you know, just as He made us, and they can't plant and grow things as we do; so they have to take what they can get, or starve to death. And surely, papa, there's enough to eat in this big and beautiful world, for all of God's creatures."

Papa whistled softly, although his face was grave; and then he bent down and kissed his little girl's forehead.

"I won't set any more traps, dear," he said.

And that evening, after Twinkle had been tucked snugly away in bed, her father walked slowly through the sweet-smelling fields to the woodchuck's hole; there lay the trap, showing plainly in the bright moonlight. He picked it up and carried it back to the barn. It was never used again.

The End

Prince Mud-Turtle

Chapter 1

Twinkle Captures the Turtle

One hot summer day Twinkle went down into the meadow to where the brook ran tinkling over its stones or rushed and whirled around the curves of the banks or floated lazily through the more wide and shallow parts. It wasn't much of a brook, to tell the facts, for there were many places where an active child could leap across it. But it was the only brook for miles around, and to Twinkle it was a never-ending source of delight. Nothing amused or refreshed the little girl more than to go wading on the pebbly bottom and let the little waves wash around her slim ankles.

There was one place, just below the pasture lot, where it was deeper; and here there were real fishes swimming about, such as "horned aces" and "chubs" and "shiners"; and once in a while you could catch a mud-turtle under the edges of the flat stones or in hollows beneath the banks. The deep part was not very big, being merely a pool, but Twinkle never waded in it, because the water would come quite up to her waist, and then she would be sure to get her skirts wet, which would mean a good scolding from mamma.

To-day she climbed the fence in the lane, just where the rickety wooden bridge crossed the brook, and at once sat down upon the grassy bank and took off her shoes and stockings. Then, wearing her sun-bonnet to shield her face from the sun, she stepped softly into the brook and stood watching the cool water rush by her legs.

It was very nice and pleasant; but Twinkle never could stand still for very long, so she began to wade slowly down the stream, keeping in the middle of the brook, and being able to see through the clear water all the best places to put her feet.

Pretty soon she had to duck her head to pass under the fence that separated the meadow from the pasture lot; but she got through all right, and then kept on down the stream, until she came close to the deep pool. She couldn't wade through this, as I have explained; so she got on dry land and crept on her hands and knees up to the edge of the bank, so as not to scare the fishes, if any were swimming in the pool.

By good luck there were several fishes in the pool to-day, and they didn't seem to notice that Twinkle was looking at them, so quiet had she been. One little fellow shone like silver when the sunshine caught his glossy sides, and the little girl watched him wiggling here and there with much delight. There was also a big, mud-colored fish that lay a long time upon the bottom without moving anything except his fins and the tip of his tail, and Twinkle also discovered a group of several small fishes not over an inch long, that always swam together in a bunch, as if they belonged to one family.

The girl watched these little creatures long and earnestly. The pool was all of the world these simple fishes would ever know. They were born here, and would die here, without ever getting away from the place, or even knowing there was a much bigger world outside of it.

After a time the child noticed that the water had become a little muddy near the edge of the bank where she lay, and as it slowly grew clear again she saw a beautiful turtle lying just under her head and against the side of the bank. It was a little bigger around than a silver dollar, and instead of its shell being

Twinkle captures the turtle

of a dull brown color, like that of all other mud-turtles she had seen, this one's back was streaked with brilliant patches of yellow and red.

"I must get that lovely turtle!" thought Twinkle; and as the water was shallow where it lay she suddenly plunged in her hand, grabbed the turtle, and flung it out of the water on to the bank, where it fell upon its back, wiggling its four fat legs desperately in an attempt to turn over.

Chapter 2

Twinkle Discovers the Turtle Can Talk

At this sudden commotion in their water, the fishes darted away and disappeared in a flash. But Twinkle didn't mind that, for all her interest was now centered in the struggling turtle.

She knelt upon the grass and bent over to watch it, and just then she thought she heard a small voice say:

"It's no use; I can't do it!" and then the turtle drew its head and legs between the shells and remained still.

"Good gracious!" said Twinkle, much astonished. Then, addressing the turtle, she asked:

"Did you say anything, a minute ago?"

There was no reply. The turtle lay as quiet as if it were dead. Twinkle thought she must have been mistaken; so she picked up the turtle and held it in the palm of her hand while she got into the water again and waded slowly back to where she had left her shoes and stockings.

When she got home she put the mud-turtle in a tub which her papa had made by sawing a barrel in two. Then she put a little water into the tub and blocked it up by putting a brick under one side, so that the turtle could either stay in the water or crawl up the inclined bottom of the tub to where it was dry, whichever he pleased. She did this because mamma said that turtles sometimes liked to stay in the water and sometimes on land, and

Twinkle's turtle could now take his choice. He couldn't climb up the steep sides of the tub and so get away, and the little girl thoughtfully placed crumbs of bread and fine bits of meat, where the turtle could get them whenever he felt hungry.

After that, Twinkle often sat for hours watching the turtle, which would crawl around the bottom of the tub, and swim in the little pool of water and eat the food placed before him in an eager and amusing way.

At times she took him in her hand and examined him closely, and then the mud-turtle would put out its little head and look at her with its bright eyes as curiously as the girl looked at him.

She had owned her turtle just a week, when she came to the tub one afternoon and held him in her hand, intending to feed her pet some scraps of meat she had brought with her. But as soon as the turtle put out its head it said to her, in a small but distinct voice:

"Good morning, Twinkle."

She was so surprised that the meat dropped from her hand, and she nearly dropped the turtle, too. But she managed to control her astonishment, and asked, in a voice that trembled a little:

"Can you talk?"

"To be sure," replied the turtle; "but only on every seventh day — which of course is every Saturday. On other days I cannot talk at all."

"Then I really must have heard you speak when I caught you; didn't I?"

"I believe you did. I was so startled at being captured that I spoke before I thought, which is a bad habit to get into. But afterward I resolved not to answer when you questioned me, for I didn't know you then, and feared it would be unwise to trust you with my secret. Even now I must ask you not to tell any one that you have a turtle that knows how to talk."

Chapter 3

The Turtle Tells of the Corrugated Giant

"Why, it's wonderful!" said Twinkle, who had listened eagerly to the turtle's speech.

"It would be wonderful, indeed, if I were but a simple turtle," was the reply.

"But aren't you a turtle?"

"Of course, so far as my outward appearance goes, I'm a common little mud-turtle," it answered; "and I think you will agree with me that it was rather clever in the Corrugated Giant to transform me into such a creature."

"What's a Corrulated Giant?" asked Twinkle, with breathless interest.

"The Corrugated Giant is a monster that is full of deep wrinkles, because he has no bones inside him to hold his flesh up properly," said the turtle. "I hated this giant, who is both wicked and cruel, I assure you; and this giant hated me in return. So, when one day I tried to destroy him, the monster transformed me into the helpless little being you see before you."

"But who were you before you were transformed?" asked the girl.

"A fairy prince named Melga, the seventh son of the fairy Queen Flutterlight, who rules all the fairies in the north part of this land."

"And how long have you been a turtle?"

"Fourteen years," replied the creature, with a deep sigh. "At least, I think it is fourteen years; but of course when one is swimming around in brooks and grubbing in the mud for food, one is apt to lose all track of time."

"I should think so, indeed," said Twinkle. "But, according to that, you're older than I am."

"Much older," declared the turtle. "I had lived about four hundred years before the Corrugated Giant turned me into a turtle."

"Was your head gray?" she asked; "and did you have white whiskers?"

"No, indeed!" said the turtle. "Fairies are always young and beautiful in appearance, no matter how many years they have lived. And, as they never die, they're bound to get pretty old sometimes, as a matter of course."

"Of course!" agreed Twinkle. "Mama has told me about the fairies. But must you always be a mud-turtle?"

"That will depend on whether you are willing to help me or not," was the answer.

"Why, it sounds just like a fairy tale in a book!" cried the little girl.

"Yes," replied the turtle, "these things have been happening ever since there were fairies, and you might expect some of our adventures would get into books. But are you willing to help me? That is the important thing just now."

"I'll do anything I can," said Twinkle.

"Then," said the turtle, "I may expect to get back to my own form again in a reasonably short time. But you must be brave, and not shrink from such a little thing as danger."

That made Twinkle look solemn.

"Of course I don't want to get hurt," she said. "My mama and papa would go di*struc*ted if anything happened to me."

"Something will happen, *sure*," declared the turtle; "but nothing that happens will hurt you in the least if you do exactly as I tell you."

"I won't have to fight that Carbolated Giant, will I?" Twinkle asked doubtfully.

"He isn't carbolated; he's corrugated. No, you won't have to fight at all. When the proper time comes I'll do the fighting myself. But you may have to come with me to the Black Mountains, in order to set me free."

"Is it far?" she asked.

"Yes; but it won't take us long to go there," answered the turtle. "Now, I'll tell you what to do and, if you follow my advice no one will ever know you've been mixed up with fairies and strange adventures."

"And Collerated Giants," she added.

"Corrugated," he corrected. "It is too late, this Saturday, to start upon our journey, so we must wait another week. But next Saturday morning you do come to me bright and early, as soon as you've had breakfast, and then I'll tell you what to do."

"All right," said Twinkle; "I won't forget."

"In the mean time, do give me a little clean water now and then. I'm a mud-turtle, sure enough; but I'm also a fairy prince, and I must say I prefer clean water."

"I'll attend to it," promised the girl.

"Now put me down and run away," continued the turtle. "It will take me all the week to think over my plans, and decide exactly what we are to do."

Chapter 4

Prince Turtle Remembers His Magic

Twinkle was as nervous as she could be during all the week that followed this strange conversation with Prince Turtle. Every day, as soon as school was out, she would run to the tub to see if the turtle was still safe — for she worried lest it should run away or disappear in some strange manner. And during school hours it was such hard work to keep her mind on her lessons that teacher scolded her more than once.

The fairy imprisoned in the turtle's form had nothing to say to her during this week, because he would not be allowed to talk again until Saturday; so the most that Twinkle could do to show her interest in the Prince was to give him the choicest food she could get and supply him with plenty of fresh, clean water.

At last the day of her adventure arrived, and as soon as she could get away from the breakfast table Twinkle ran out to the tub. There was her fairy turtle, safe as could be, and as she leaned over the tub he put out his head and called "Good morning!" in his small, shrill voice.

"Good morning," she replied.

"Are you still willing and ready to assist me?" asked the turtle.

"To be sure," said Twinkle.

"Then take me in your hand," said he.

So she picked him out of the tub and placed him upon her hand. And the turtle said:

"Now pay strict attention, and do exactly as I tell you, and all will be well. In the first place, we want to get to the Black Mountains; so you must repeat after me these words: '*Uller; aller; iller; oller!*'"

"Uller; aller; iller; oller!" said Twinkle.

The next minute it seemed as though a gale of wind had struck her. It blew so strongly against her eyes that she could not see; so she covered her face with one arm while with the other hand she held fast to the turtle. Her skirts fluttered so wildly that it seemed as if they would tear themselves from her body, and her sun-bonnet, not being properly fastened, was gone in a minute.

But it didn't last long, fortunately. After a few moments the wind stopped, and she found she could breathe again. Then she looked around her and drew another long breath, for instead of being in the back yard at home she stood on the side of a beautiful mountain, and spread before her were the loveliest green valleys she had ever beheld.

"Well, we're here," said the turtle, in a voice that sounded as if he were well pleased. "I thought I hadn't forgotten my fairy wisdom."

"Where are we?" asked the child.

"In the Black Mountains, of course," was the reply. "We've come a good way, but it didn't take us long to arrive, did it?"

"No, indeed," she answered, still gazing down the mountain side at the flower-strewn grass-land of the valleys.

"This," said the turtle, sticking his little head out of the shell as far as it would go, "is the realm of the fairies, where I used to dwell. Those beautiful palaces you see yonder are inhabited

"Rub your eyelids with it"

by Queen Flutterlight and my people, and that grim castle at your left, standing on the side of the mountain, is where the Corrugated Giant lives."

"I don't see anything!" exclaimed Twinkle; "that is, nothing but the valleys and the flowers and grass."

"True; I had forgotten that these things are invisible to your mortal eyes. But it is necessary that you should see all clearly, if you are going to rescue me from this terrible form and restore me to my natural shape. Now, put me down upon the ground, for I must search for a particular plant whose leaf has a magic virtue."

So Twinkle put him down, and the little turtle began running around here and there, looking carefully at the different plants that grew amongst the grass on the mountain side. But his legs were so short and his shell-covered body so heavy, that he couldn't move very fast; so presently he called for her to pick him up again, and hold him close to the ground while she walked among the plants. She did this, and after what seemed a long search the turtle suddenly cried out:

"Stop! Here it is! This is the plant I want."

"Which — this?" asked the girl, touching a broad green leaf.

"Yes. Pluck the leaf from the stem and rub your eyelids with it."

She obeyed, and having rubbed her lids well with the leaf, she again opened her eyes and beheld the real Fairyland.

Chapter 5

Twinkle Promises to Be Brave

In the center of the valley was a great cluster of palaces that appeared to be built of crystal and silver and mother-of-pearl, and golden filigree-work. So dainty and beautiful were these fairy dwellings that Twinkle had no doubt for an instant but that she gazed upon fairyland. She could almost see, from the far mountain upon which she stood, the airy, gauze-winged forms of the fairies themselves, floating gently amidst their pretty palaces and moving gracefully along the jeweled streets.

But another sight now attracted her attention — a big, gray, ugly looking castle standing frowning on the mountain side at her left. It overlooked the lovely city of palaces like a dark cloud on the edge of a blue sky, and the girl could not help giving a shudder as she saw it. All around the castle was a high fence of iron spikes.

"That fence is enchanted," said the turtle, as if he knew she was looking at it; "and no fairy can pass it, because the power to prevent it has been given to the giant. But a mortal has never been forbidden to pass the fence, for no one ever supposed that a mortal would come here or be able to see it. That is the reason I have brought you to this place, and the reason why you alone are able to help me."

"Gracious!" cried Twinkle; "must I meet the Carbonated Giant?"

"He's corrugated," said the turtle.

"I know he's something dreadful," she wailed, "because he's so hard to pronounce."

"You will surely have to meet him," declared the turtle; "but do not fear, I will protect you from all harm."

"Well, a Corralated Giant's a mighty big person," said the girl, doubtfully, "and a mud-turtle isn't much of a fighter. I guess I'll go home."

"That is impossible," declared the turtle. "You are too far from home ever to get back without my help, so you may as well be good and obedient."

"What must I do?" she asked.

"We will wait until it is nearly noon, when the giant will put his pot on the fire to boil his dinner. We can tell the right time by watching the smoke come out of his chimney. Then you must march straight up to the castle and into the kitchen where the giant is at work, and throw me quickly into the boiling kettle. That is all that you will be required to do."

"I never could do it!" declared Twinkle.

"Why not?"

"You'd be scalded to death, and then I'd be a murderer!"

"Nonsense!" said the turtle, peevishly. "I know what I'm doing, and if you obey me I'll not be scalded but an instant; for then I'll resume my own form. Remember that I'm a fairy, and fairies can't be killed so easily as you seem to think."

"Won't it hurt you?" she inquired.

"Only for a moment; but the reward will be so great that I won't mind an instant's pain. Will you do this favor for me?"

"I'll try," replied Twinkle, gravely.

"Then I will be very grateful," said Prince Turtle, "and agree to afterward send you home safe and sound, and as quickly as you came."

97

Chapter 6

Twinkle Meets the Corrugated Giant

"And now, while we are waiting," continued the fairy turtle, "I want to find a certain flower that has wonderful powers to protect mortals from any injury. Not that I fear I shall be unable to take care of you, but it's just as well to be on the safe side."

"Better," said Twinkle, earnestly. "Where's the flower?"

"We'll hunt for it," replied the turtle.

So holding him in her hand in such a way that he could see all the flowers that grew, the girl began wandering over the mountain side, and everything was so beautiful around her that she would have been quite contented and happy had not the gray castle been before her to remind her constantly that she must face the terrible giant who lived within it.

They found the flower at last — a pretty pink blossom that looked like a double daisy, but must have been something else, because a daisy has no magic power that I ever heard of. And when it was found, the turtle told her to pick the flower and pin it fast to the front of her dress; which she did.

By that time the smoke began to roll out of the giant's chimney in big black clouds; so the fairy turtle said the giant must be getting dinner, and the pot would surely be boiling by the time they got to the castle.

Twinkle couldn't help being a little afraid to approach the

giant's stronghold, but she tried to be brave, and so stepped along briskly until she came to the fence of iron spikes.

"You must squeeze through between two of the spikes," said the turtle.

She didn't think it could possibly be done; but to her surprise it was quite easy, and she managed to squeeze through the fence without even tearing her dress. Then she walked up a great driveway, which was lined with white skulls of many sheep which the giant had eaten, to the front door of the castle, which stood ajar.

"Go in," said the turtle; so she boldly entered and passed down a high arched hall toward a room in the rear.

"This is the kitchen," said the turtle. "Enter quickly, go straight to the kettle, and throw me into the boiling water."

Twinkle entered quickly enough, but then she stopped short with a cry of amazement; for there before her stood the ugly giant, blowing the fire with an immense pair of bellows.

Chapter 7

Prince Mud-Turtle Becomes Prince Melga

T he giant was as big around as ten men, and as tall as two; but, having no bones, he seemed pushed together, so that his skin wrinkled up like the sides of an accordeon, or a photograph camera, even his face being so wrinkled that his nose stuck out between two folds of flesh and his eyes from between two more. In one end of the kitchen was the great fireplace, above which hung an iron kettle with a big iron spoon in it. And at the other end was a table set for dinner.

As the giant was standing between the kettle and Twinkle, she could not do as the turtle had commanded, and throw him into the pot. So she hesitated, wondering how to obey the fairy. Just then the giant happened to turn around and see her.

"By the whiskers of Gammarog — who was one of my ancestors that was killed by Jack the Giant-Killer!" he cried, but in a very mild voice for so big a person. "Whom have we here?"

"I'm Twinkle," said the girl, drawing a long breath.

"Then, to pay you for your folly in entering my castle, I will make you my slave, and some day, if you're not good, I'll feed you to my seventeen-headed dog. I never eat little girls myself. I prefer mutton."

Twinkle's heart almost stopped beating when she heard these awful words. All she could do was to stand still and look implor-

Twinkle meets the Corrugated Giant

ingly at the giant. But she held the fairy mud-turtle clasped tight in her hand, so that the monster couldn't see it.

"Well, what are you staring at?" shouted the Corrugated Giant, angrily. "Blow up that fire this instant, slave!"

He stood aside for her to pass, and Twinkle ran at once to the fireplace. The pot was now before her, and within easy reach, and it was bubbling hot.

In an instant she reached out her hand and tossed the turtle into the boiling water; and then, with a cry of horror at her own action, she drew back to see what would happen.

The turtle was a fairy, all right; and he had known very well the best way to break the enchantment his enemy had put upon him. For no sooner had Twinkle tossed him into the boiling pot than a great hissing was heard, and a cloud of steam hid for an instant the fireplace. Then, as it cleared away, a handsome young prince stepped forward, fully armed; for the turtle was again a fairy, and the kettle had changed into a strong shield which he bore upon his left arm, and the iron spoon was now a long and glittering sword.

Chapter 8

Twinkle Receives a Medal

T he giant gave a roar like that of a baby bull when he saw Prince Melga standing before him, and in a twinkling he had caught up a big club that stood near and began whirling it over his head. But before it could descend, the prince ran at him and stuck his sword as far as it would go into the corrugated body of the giant. Again the monster roared and tried to fight; but the sword had hurt him badly, and the prince pushed it into the evil creature again and again, until the end came, and his corrugated enemy rolled over upon the floor quite dead.

Then the fairy turned to Twinkle, and kneeling before her he kissed her hand.

"Thank you very much," he said, in a sweet voice, "for setting me free. You are a very brave little girl!"

"I'm not so sure about that," she answered. "I was dreadfully scared!"

Now he took her hand and let her from the castle; and she didn't have to squeeze through the fence again, because the fairy had only to utter a magic word and the gate flew open. And when they turned to look back, the castle of the Corrugated Giant, with all that it had contained, had vanished from sight, never to be seen again by either mortal or fairy eyes. For that was sure to happen whenever the giant was dead.

The prince led Twinkle into the valley where the fairy palaces stood, and told all his people, when they crowded around to welcome him, how kind the little girl had been to him, and how her courage had enabled him to defeat the giant and to regain his proper form. And all the fairies praised Twinkle with kind words, and the lovely Queen Flutterlight, who seemed altogether too young to be the mother of the handsome prince, gave to the child a golden medal with a tiny mud-turtle engraved upon one side of it.

Then, after a fine feast had been prepared, and the little girl had eaten all she could of the fairy sweetmeats, she told Prince Melga she would like to go home again.

"Very well," said he. "Don't forget me, Twinkle, although we probably shall never meet again. I'll send you home quite as safely as you came; but as your eyes have been rubbed with the magic maita-leaf, you will doubtless always see many strange sights that are hidden from other mortals."

"I don't mind," said Twinkle.

Then she bade good-bye to the fairies, and the prince spoke a magic word. There was another rush of wind, and when it had passed Twinkle found herself once more in the back yard at home.

As she sat upon the grass rubbing her eyes and wondering at the strange adventure that had befallen her, mama came out upon the back porch and said:

"Your turtle has crawled out of the tub and run away."

"Yes," said Twinkle, "I know; and I'm glad of it!"

But she kept her secret to herself.

Twinkle's Enchantment

Chapter 1

Twinkle Enters the Big Gulch

One afternoon Twinkle decided to go into the big gulch and pick some blueberries for papa's supper. She had on her blue gingham dress and her blue sun-bonnet, and there were stout shoes upon her feet. So she took her tin pail and started out.

"Be back in time for supper," called mamma from the kitchen porch.

"'Course," said Twinkle, as she trotted away. "I'm not hungry now, but I'll be hungry 'nough when supper-time comes. 'Course I'll be back!"

The side of the gulch was but a little way from the house. It was like a big ditch, only the sides were not too steep to crawl down; and in the middle of the gulch were rolling hills and deep gullies, all covered with wild bushes and vines and a few flowering plants — very rare in this part of the country.

Twinkle hadn't lived very long in this section of Dakota, for her father had just bought the new farm that lay beside the gulch. So the big ditch was a great delight to her, and she loved to wander through it and pick the berries and flowers that never grew on the plains above.

To-day she crept carefully down the path back of the house and soon reached the bottom of the gulch. Then she began to search for the berries; but all were gone in the places where she had picked them before; so she found she must go further along.

She sat down to rest for a time, and by and by she happened to look up at the other side and saw a big cluster of bushes hanging full of ripe blueberries — just about half way up the opposite bank.

She had never gone so far before, but if she wanted the berries for papa's supper she knew she must climb up the slope and get them; so she rose to her feet and began to walk in that direction. It was all new to the little girl, and seemed to her like a beautiful fairyland; but she had no idea that the gulch was enchanted. Soon a beetle crawled across her path, and as she stopped to let it go by, she heard it say:

"Look out for the line of enchantment! You'll soon cross it, if you don't watch out."

"What line of enchantment?" asked Twinkle.

"It's almost under your nose," replied the little creature.

"I don't see anything at all," she said, after looking closely.

"Of course you don't, said the beetle. "It isn't a mark, you know, that any one can see with their eyes; but it's a line of enchantment, just the same, and whoever steps over it is sure to see strange things and have strange adventures."

"I don't mind that," said Twinkle.

"Well, I don't mind if you don't," returned the beetle, and by that time he had crept across the path and disappeared underneath a big rock.

Twinkle went on, without being at all afraid. If the beetle spoke truly, and there really was an invisible line that divided the common, real world from an enchanted country, she was very eager to cross it, as any little girl might well be. And then it occurred to her that she must have crossed the enchanted line before she met the beetle, for otherwise she wouldn't have understood his language, or known what he was talking about. Children don't talk with beetles in the real world, as Twinkle knew very well, and she was walking along soberly, thinking this over, when suddenly a voice cried out to her:

"Be careful!"

Chapter 2

The Rolling Stone

Of course Twinkle stopped then, and looked around to see who had spoken. But no one was anywhere in sight. So she started on again.

"Look out, or you'll step on me!" cried the voice a second time.

She looked at her feet very carefully. There was nothing near them but a big round stone that was about the size of her head, and a prickly thistle that she never would step on if she could possibly help it.

"Who's talking?" she asked.

"Why, *I'm* talking," answered the voice. "Who do you suppose it is?"

"I don't know," said Twinkle. "I just can't see anybody at all."

"Then you must be blind," said the voice. "I'm the Rolling Stone, and I'm about two inches from your left toes."

"The Rolling Stone!"

"That's it. That's me. I'm the Rolling Stone that gathers no moss."

"You can't be," said Twinkle, sitting down in the path and looking carefully at the stone.

"Why not?"

"Because you don't roll," she said. "You're a stone, of course; I can see that, all right. But you're not rolling."

Twinkle looks carefully at the stone

"How silly!" replied the Stone. "I don't have to roll every minute to be a Rolling Stone, do I?"

"Of course you do," answered Twinkle. "If you don't roll you're just a common, *still* stone."

"Well, I declare!" exclaimed the Stone; "you don't seem to understand anything. You're a Talking Girl, are you not?"

"To be sure I am," said Twinkle.

"But you don't talk every minute, do you?"

"Mama says I do," she answered.

"But you don't. You're sometimes quiet, aren't you?"

" 'Course I am."

"That's the way with me. Sometimes I roll, and so I'm called the Rolling Stone. Sometimes you talk, and so you're the Talking Girl."

"No; I'm Twinkle," she said.

"That doesn't sound like a name," remarked the Stone.

"It's what papa calls me, anyway," explained the girl. Then, thinking she had lingered long enough, she added:

"I'm going up the hill to pick those berries. Since you can roll, suppose you go with me."

"What! Up hill?" exclaimed the Stone.

"Why not?" asked Twinkle.

"Who ever heard of a stone rolling up hill? It's unnatural!"

"Any stone can roll down hill," said the child. "If you can't roll up hill, you're no better than a common cobble-stone."

"Oh, I can roll up hill if I have to," declared the Stone, peevishly. "But it's hard work, and nearly breaks my back."

"I can't see that you have any back," said Twinkle.

"Why, I'm all back," replied the Stone. When *your* back aches, it's only a part of you. But when *my* back aches, it's all of me except the middle."

"The middle ache is the worst of all," said Twinkle, solemnly.

"Well, if you don't want to go," she added, jumping up, "I'll say good-bye."

"Anything to be sociable," said the Stone, sighing deeply. "I'll go along and keep you company. But it's lots easier to roll down than it is to roll up, I assure you!"

"Why, you're a reg'lar grumbler!" exclaimed Twinkle.

"That's because I lead a hard life," returned the Stone, dismally. "But don't let us quarrel; it is so seldom I get a chance to talk with one of my own standing in society."

"You can't have any standing, without feet," declared Twinkle, shaking her head at the Stone.

"One can have *under*standing, at least," was the answer; "and understanding is the best standing any person can have."

"Perhaps that is true," said the child, thoughtfully; "but I'm glad I have legs, just the same."

Chapter 3

Some Queer Acquaintances

"Wait a minute!" implored a small voice, and the girl noticed a yellow butterfly that had just settled down upon the stone. "Aren't you the child from the farm?"

"To be sure," she answered, much amused to hear the butterfly speak.

"Then can you tell me if your mother expects to churn to-day," said the pretty creature, slowly folding and unfolding its dainty wings.

"Why do you want to know?"

"If she churns to-day, I'll fly over to the house and try to steal some butter. But if your mother isn't going to churn, I'll fly down into the gulch and rob a bees' nest I know of."

"Why do you rob and steal?" inquired Twinkle.

"It's the only way I can get my living," said the butterfly. "Nobody ever gives me anything, and so I have to take what I want."

"Do you like butter?"

"Of course I do! That's why we are called butterflies, you know. I prefer butter to anything else, and I have heard that in some countries the children always leave a little dish of butter on the window-sill so that we may help ourselves whenever we are hungry. I wish I had been born in such a country."

"Mother won't churn until Saturday," said Twinkle. "I know, 'cause I've got to help her, and I just hate butter-making!"

"Then I won't go to the farm to-day," replied the butterfly.

"Good-bye, little girl. If you think of it, leave a dish of butter around where I can get at it."

"All right," said Twinkle, and the butterfly waved its wings and fluttered through the air into the gulch below.

Then the girl started up the hill and the Stone rolled slowly beside her, groaning and grumbling because the ground was so rough.

Presently she noticed running across the path a tiny Book, not much bigger than a postage-stamp. It had two slender legs, like those of a bumble-bee, and upon these it ran so fast that all the leaves fluttered wildly, the covers being half open.

"What's that?" asked Twinkle, looking after the book in surprise.

"That is a little Learning," answered the Stone. "Look out for it, for they say it's a dangerous thing."

"It's gone already," said Twinkle.

"Let it go. Nobody wants it, that I know of. Just help me over this bump, will you?"

So she rolled the Stone over the little hillock, and just as she did so her attention was attracted by a curious noise that sounded like "Pop! pop! pop!"

"What's that?" she inquired, hesitating to advance.

"Only a weasel," answered the Stone. "Stand still a minute, and you'll see him. Whenever he thinks he's alone, and there's no one to hear, 'pop' goes the weasel."

Sure enough, a little animal soon crossed their path, making the funny noise at every step. But as soon as he saw that Twinkle was staring at him he stopped popping and rushed into a bunch of tall grass and hid himself.

And now they were almost at the berry-bushes, and Twinkle trotted so fast that the Rolling Stone had hard work to keep up with her. But when she got to the bushes she found a flock of strange birds sitting upon them and eating up the berries as fast

The birds of one feather

as they could. The birds were not much bigger than robins, and were covered with a soft, velvety skin instead of with feathers, and they had merry black eyes and long, slender beaks curving downward from their noses, which gave to their faces a saucy expression. The lack of usual feathers might not have surprised Twinkle so much had she not noticed upon the tail of each bird one single, solitary feather of great length, which was certainly a remarkable thing.

"I know what they are," she said, nodding her head wisely; "they're birds of a feather."

At this the birds burst into a chorus of laughter, and one of them said:

"Perhaps you think that's why we flock together."

"Well, isn't that the reason?" she asked.

"Not a bit of it, declared the bird. The reason we flock together is because we're too proud to mix with common birds, who have feathers all over them."

"I should think you'd be ashamed, 'cause you're so naked," she returned.

"The fact is, Twinkle," said another bird, as he pecked at a blueberry and swallowed it, "the common things in this world don't amount to much. There are millions of birds on earth, but only a few of us that have but one feather. In my opinion, if you had but one hair upon your head you'd be much prettier."

"I'd be more 'strord'nary, I'm sure," said Twinkle, using the biggest word she could think of.

"There's no accounting for tastes," remarked the Rolling Stone, which had just arrived at Twinkle's side after a hard roll up the path. "For my part, I haven't either hair or feathers, and I'm glad of it."

The birds laughed again, at this, and as they had eaten all the berries they cared for, they now flew into the air and disappeared.

Chapter 4

The Dancing Bear

"Really," said Twinkle as she began picking the berries and putting them into her pail, "I didn't know so many things could talk."

"It's because you are in the part of the gulch that's enchanted," answered the Rolling Stone. "When you get home again, you'll think this is all a dream."

"I wonder if it isn't!" she suddenly cried, stopping to look around, and then feeling of herself carefully. "It's usually the way in all the fairy stories that papa reads to me. I don't remember going to sleep any time; but perhaps I did, after all."

"Don't let it worry you," said the Stone, making a queer noise that Twinkle thought was meant for a laugh. "If you wake up, you'll be sorry you didn't dream longer; and if you find you haven't been asleep, this will be a wonderful adventure."

"That's true enough," the girl answered, and again began filling her pail with the berries. "When I tell mama all this, she won't believe a word of it. And papa will laugh and pinch my cheek, and say I'm like Alice in Wonderland, or Dorothy in the Land of Oz."

Just then she noticed something big and black coming around the bushes from the other side, and her heart beat a good deal faster when she saw before her a great bear standing upon his rear legs beside her.

He had a little red cap on his head that was kept in place by a band of rubber elastic. His eyes were small, but round and sparkling, and there seemed to be a smile upon his face, for his white teeth showed in two long rows.

"Don't be afraid," called out the Rolling Stone; "it's only the Dancing Bear."

"Why should the child be afraid?" asked the bear, speaking in a low, soft tone that reminded her of the purring of a kitten. "No one ever heard of a Dancing Bear hurting anybody. We're about the most harmless things in the world."

"Are you really a Dancing Bear?" asked Twinkle, curiously.

"I am, my dear," he replied, bowing low and then folding his arms proudly as he leaned against a big rock that was near. "I wish there was some one here who could tell you what a fine dancer I am. It wouldn't be modest for me to praise myself, you know."

"I s'pose not," said Twinkle. "But if you're a Dancing Bear, why don't you dance?"

"There it is again!" cried the Rolling Stone. "This girl Twinkle wants to keep every body moving. She wouldn't believe, at first, that I was a Rolling Stone, because I was lying quiet just then. And now she won't believe you're a Dancing Bear, because you don't eternally keep dancing."

"Well, there's some sense in that, after all," declared the Bear. "I'm only a Dancing Bear while I'm dancing, to speak the exact truth; and you're only a Rolling Stone while your rolling."

"I beg to disagree with you," returned the Stone, in a cold voice.

"Well, don't let us quarrel, on any account," said the Bear. "I invite you both to come to my cave and see me dance. Then Twinkle will be sure I'm a Dancing Bear."

"I haven't filled my pail yet," said the little girl, "and I've got to get enough berries for papa's supper."

"I'll help you," replied the Bear, politely; and at once he began to pick berries and to put them into Twinkle's pail. His big paws looked very clumsy and awkward, but it was astonishing how many blueberries the bear could pick with them. Twinkle had hard work to keep up with him, and almost before she realized how fast they had worked, the little pail was full and overflowing with fine, plump berries.

"And now," said the Bear, "I will show you the way to my cave."

He took her hand in his soft paw and began leading her along the side of the steep hill, while the Stone rolled busily along just behind them. But they had not gone far before Twinkle's foot slipped, and in trying to save herself from falling she pushed hard against the Stone and tumbled it from the pathway.

"Now you've done it!" growled the Stone, excitedly, as it whirled around. "Here I go, for I've lost my balance and I can't help myself!"

Even as he spoke the big round stone was flying down the side of the gulch, bumping against the hillocks and bits of rock — sometimes leaping into the air and then clinging close to the ground, but going faster and faster every minute.

"Dear me," said Twinkle, looking after it; "I'm afraid the Rolling Stone will get hurt."

"No danger of that," replied the Bear. "It's as hard as a rock, and not a thing in the gulch could hurt it a bit. But our friend would have to roll a long time to get back here again, so we won't wait. Come along, my dear."

He held out his paw again, and Twinkle took it with one of her hands while she carried the pail with the other, and so managed to get over the rough ground very easily.

Chapter 5

The Cave of the Waterfall

B efore long they came to the entrance to the cave, and as it looked dark and gloomy from without Twinkle drew back and said she guessed she wouldn't go in.

"But it's quite light inside," said the bear, "and there's a pretty waterfall there, too. Don't be afraid, Twinkle; I'll take good care of you."

So the girl plucked up courage and permitted him to lead her into the cave; and then she was glad she had come, instead of being a 'fraid-cat. For the place was big and roomy, and there were many cracks in the roof, that admitted plenty of light and air. Around the side walls were several pairs of big ears, which seemed to have been carved out of the rock. These astonished the little girl.

"What are the ears for?" she asked.

"Don't walls have ears where you live?" returned the Bear, as if surprised.

"I've heard they do," she answered, "but I've never seen any before."

At the back of the cave was a little, tinkling waterfall, that splashed into a pool beneath with a sound that was very like music. Near this was a square slab of rock, a little raised above the level of the floor.

"Kindly take a seat, my dear," said the bear, "and I'll try to amuse you, and at the same time prove that I can dance."

So to the music of the waterfall the bear began dancing. He climbed upon the flat stone, made a graceful bow to Twinkle, and then balanced himself first upon one foot and then upon the other, and swung slowly around in a circle, and then back again.

"How do you like it?" he asked.

"I don't care much for it," said Twinkle. "I believe I could do better myself."

"But you are not a bear," he answered. "Girls ought to dance better than bears, you know. But not every bear can dance. If I had a hand-organ to make the music, instead of this waterfall, I might do better."

"Then I wish you had one," said the girl.

The Bear began dancing again, and this time he moved more rapidly and shuffled his feet in quite a funny manner. He almost fell off the slab once or twice, so anxious was he to prove he could dance. And once he tripped over his own foot, which made Twinkle laugh.

Just as he was finishing his dance a strange voice cried out:

"For bear!" and a green monkey sprang into the cave and threw a big rock at the performer. It knocked the bear off the slab, and he fell into the pool of water at the foot of the waterfall, and was dripping wet when he scrambled out again.

The Dancing Bear gave a big growl and ran as fast as he could after the monkey, finally chasing him out of the cave. Twinkle picked up her pail of berries and followed, and when she got into the sunshine again on the side of the hill she saw the monkey and the bear hugging each other tight, and growling and chattering in a way that showed they were angry with each other and not on pleasant terms.

"You *will* throw rocks at me, will you?" shouted the Bear.

The green monkey makes mischief

"I will if I get the chance," replied the monkey. "Wasn't that a fine, straight shot? and didn't you go plump into the water, though?" and he shrieked with laughter.

Just then they fell over in a heap, and began rolling down the hill.

"Let go!" yelled the Bear.

"Let go, yourself!" screamed the monkey.

But neither of them did let go, so they rolled faster and faster down the hill, and the last that Twinkle saw of them they were bounding among the bushes at the very bottom of the big gulch.

Chapter 6

Prince Nimble

"G ood gracious!" said the little girl, looking around her; "I'm as good as lost in this strange place, and I don't know in what direction to go to get home again."

So she sat down on the grass and tried to think which way she had come, and which way she ought to return in order to get across the gulch to the farm-house.

"If the Rolling Stone was here, he might tell me," she said aloud. "But I'm all alone."

"Oh, no, you're not," piped a small, sweet voice. "I'm here, and I know much more than the Rolling Stone does."

Twinkle looked this way and then that, very carefully, in order to see who had spoken, and at last she discovered a pretty grasshopper perched upon a long blade of grass nearby.

"Did I hear you speak?" she inquired.

"Yes," replied the grasshopper. "I'm Prince Nimble, the hoppiest hopper in Hoptown."

"Where is that?" asked the child.

"Why, Hoptown is near the bottom of the gulch, in that thick patch of grass you see yonder. It's on your way home, so I'd be pleased to have you visit it."

"Won't I step on some of you?" she asked.

"Not if you are careful," replied Prince Nimble. "Grasshoppers don't often get stepped on. We're pretty active, you know."

"All right," said Twinkle. "I'd like to see a grasshopper village."

"Then follow me, and I'll guide you," said Nimble, and at once he leaped from the blade of grass and landed at least six feet away.

Twinkle got up and followed, keeping her eye on the pretty Prince, who leaped so fast that she had to trot to keep up with him. Nimble would wait on some clump of grass or bit of rock until the girl came up, and then away he'd go again.

"How far is it?" Twinkle once asked him.

"About a mile and a half," was the answer; "we'll soon be there, for you are as good as a mile, and I'm good for the half-mile."

"How do you figure that out?" asked Twinkle.

"Why, I've always heard that a miss is as good as a mile, and you're a miss, are you not?"

"Not yet," she answered; "I'm only a little girl. But papa will be sure to miss me if I don't get home to supper."

Chapter 7

The Grasshoppers' Hop

T winkle now began to fear she wouldn't get home to supper, for the sun started to sink into the big prairie, and in the golden glow it left behind, the girl beheld most beautiful palaces and castles suspended in the air just above the hollow in which she stood. Splendid banners floated from the peaks and spires of these magnificent buildings, and all the windows seemed of silver and all the roofs of gold.

"What city is that?" she asked, standing still, in amazement.

"That isn't any city," replied the grasshopper. "They are only Castles in the Air — very pretty to look at, but out of everybody's reach. Come along, my little friend; we're almost at Hoptown."

So Twinkle walked on, and before long Prince Nimble paused on the stem of a hollyhock and said:

"Now, sit down carefully, right where you are, and you will be able to watch my people. It is the night of our regular hop — if you listen you can hear the orchestra tuning up."

She sat down, as he bade her, and tried to listen, but only heard a low whirr and rattle like the noise of a beetle's wings.

"That's the drummer," said Prince Nimble. "He is very clever, indeed."

"Good gracious! It's night," said Twinkle, with a start. "I ought to be at home and in bed this very minute!"

"Never mind," said the grasshopper; "you can sleep any time, but this is our annual ball, and it's a great privilege to witness it."

Suddenly the grass all around them became brilliantly lighted, as if from a thousand tiny electric lamps. Twinkle looked closely, and saw that a vast number of fire-flies had formed a circle around them, and were illuminating the scene of the ball.

In the center of the circle were assembled hundreds of grasshoppers, of all sizes. The small ones were of a delicate green color, and the middle-sized ones of a deeper green, while the biggest ones were a yellowish brown.

But the members of the orchestra interested Twinkle more than anything else. They were seated upon the broad top of a big toadstool at one side, and the musicians were all beetles and big-bugs. A fat water-beetle played a bass fiddle as big and fat as himself, and two pretty ladybugs played the violins. A scarab, brightly colored with scarlet and black, tooted upon a long horn, and a sand-beetle made the sound of a drum with its wings. Then there was a coleopto, making shrill sounds like a flute — only of course Twinkle didn't know the names of these beetles, and thought they were all just "bugs."

When the orchestra began to play, the music was more pleasing than you might suppose; anyway, the grasshoppers liked it, for they commenced at once to dance.

The antics of the grasshoppers made Twinkle laugh more than once, for the way they danced was to hop around in a circle, and jump over each other, and then a lady grasshopper and a gentleman grasshopper would take hold of hands and stand on their long rear legs and swing partners until it made the girl dizzy just to watch them.

Sometimes two of them would leap at once, and knock against each other in the air, and then go tumbling to the ground, where the other dancers tripped over them. She saw

Prince Nimble dancing away with the others, and his partner was a lovely green grasshopper with sparkling black eyes and wings that were like velvet. They didn't bump into as many of the others as some did, and Twinkle thought they danced very gracefully indeed.

And now, while the merriment was at its height, and waiter-grasshoppers were passing around refreshments that looked like grass seeds covered with thick molasses, a big cat suddenly jumped into the circle.

At once all the lights went out, for the fire-flies fled in every direction; but in the darkness Twinkle thought she could still hear the drone of the big bass fiddle and the flute-like trill of the ladybugs.

The next thing Twinkle knew, some one was shaking her shoulder.

"Wake up, dear," said her mother's voice. "It's nearly supper-time, and papa's waiting for you. And I see you haven't picked a single blueberry."

"Why, I picked 'em, all right," replied Twinkle, sitting up and first rubbing her eyes and then looking gravely at her empty tin pail. "They were all in the pail a few minutes ago. I wonder whatever became of them!"

Sugar-Loaf Mountain

❧

Chapter 1

The Golden Key

Twinkle had come to visit her old friend Chubbins, whose mother was now teaching school in a little town at the foot of the Ozark Mountains, in Arkansas. Twinkle's own home was in Dakota, so the mountains that now towered around her made her open her eyes in wonder.

Near by — so near, in fact, that she thought she might almost reach out her arm and touch it — was Sugar-Loaf Mountain, round and high and big. And a little to the south was Backbone Mountain, and still farther along a peak called Crystal Mountain.

The very next day after her arrival Twinkle asked Chubbins to take her to see the mountain; and so the boy, who was about her own age, got his mother to fill for them a basket of good things to eat, and away they started, hand in hand, to explore the mountain-side.

It was farther to Sugar-Loaf Mountain than Twinkle had thought, and by the time they reached the foot of the great mound, the rocky sides of which were covered with bushes and small trees, they were both rather tired by the walk.

"Let's eat something," suggested Chubbins.

"I'm willing," said Twinkle.

So they climbed up a little way, to where some big rocks lay flat upon the mountain, and sat themselves down upon a slab of rock while they rested and ate some of the sandwiches and cake.

"Why do they call it 'Sugar-Loaf'?" asked the girl, looking far up to the top of the mountain.

"I don't know," replied Chubbins.

"It's a queer name," said Twinkle, thoughtfully.

"That's so," agreed the boy. "They might as well have called it 'gingerbread' or 'rock-salt,' or 'tea-biscuit.' They call mountains funny names, don't they?"

"Seems as if they do," said Twinkle.

They had been sitting upon the edge of one big flat rock, with their feet resting against another that was almost as large. These rocks appeared to have been there for ages, — as if some big giants in olden days had tossed them carelessly down and then gone away and left them. Yet as the children pushed their feet against this one, the heavy mass suddenly began to tremble and then slide downward.

"Look out!" cried the girl, frightened to see the slab of rock move. "We'll fall and get hurt!"

But they clung to the rock upon which they sat and met with no harm whatever. Nor did the big slab of stone below them move very far from its original position. It merely slid downward a few feet, and when they looked at the place where it had been they discovered what seemed to be a small iron door, built into the solid stone underneath, and now shown to their view by the moving of the upper rock.

"Why, it's a door!" exclaimed Twinkle.

Chubbins got down upon his knees and examined the door carefully. There was a ring in it that seemed to be a handle, and he caught hold of it and pulled as hard as he could. But it wouldn't move.

"It's locked, Twink," he said.

"What do you 'spose is under it?" she asked.

"Maybe it's a treasure"

"Maybe it's a treasure!" answered Chubbins, his eyes big with interest.

"Well, Chub, we can't get it, anyway," said the practical Twinkle; "so let's climb the mountain."

She got down from her seat and approached the door, and as she did so she struck a small bit of rock with her foot and sent it tumbling down the hill. Then she stopped short with a cry of wonder, for under the stone she had kicked away was a little hole in the rock, and within this they saw a small golden key.

"Perhaps," she said, eagerly, as she stooped to pick up the key, "this will unlock the iron door."

"Let's try it!" cried the boy.

Chapter 2

Through the Tunnel

They examined the door carefully, and at last found near the center of it a small hole. Twinkle put the golden key into this and found that it fitted exactly. But it took all of Chubbins's strength to turn the key in the rusty lock. Yet finally it did turn, and they heard the noise of bolts shooting back, so they both took hold of the ring, and pulling hard together, managed to raise the iron door on its hinges.

All they saw was a dark tunnel, with stone steps leading down into the mountain.

"No treasure here," said the little girl.

"P'raps it's farther in," replied Chubbins. "Shall we go down?"

"Won't it be dangerous?" she asked.

"Don't know," said Chubbins, honestly. "It's been years and years since this door was opened. You can see for yourself. That rock must have covered it up a long time."

"There must be *something* inside," she declared, "or there wouldn't be any door, or any steps."

"That's so," answered Chubbins. "I'll go down and see. You wait."

"No; I'll go too," said Twinkle. "I'd be just as scared waiting outside as I would be in. And I'm bigger than you are, Chub."

"You're taller, but you're only a month older, Twink; so don't you put on airs. And I'm the strongest."

"We'll both go," she decided; "and then if we find the treasure we'll divide."

"All right; come on!"

Forgetting their basket, which they left upon the rocks, they crept through the little doorway and down the steps. There were only seven steps in all, and then came a narrow but level tunnel that led straight into the mountain-side. It was dark a few feet from the door, but the children resolved to go on. Taking hold of hands, so as not to get separated, and feeling the sides of the passages to guide them, they walked a long way into the black tunnel.

Twinkle was just about to say they'd better go back, when the passage suddenly turned, and far ahead of them shone a faint light. This encouraged them, and they went on faster, hoping they would soon come to the treasure.

"Keep it up, Twink," said the boy. "It's no use going home yet."

"We must be almost in the middle of Sugar-Loaf Mountain," she answered.

"Oh, no; it's an awful big mountain," said he. "But we've come quite a way, haven't we?"

"I guess mama'd scold, if she knew where we are."

"Mamas," said Chubbins, "shouldn't know everything, 'cause they'd only worry. And if we don't get hurt I can't see as there's any harm done."

"But we mustn't be naughty, Chub."

"The only thing that's naughty," he replied, "is doing what you're told not to do. And no one told us not to go into the middle of Sugar-Loaf Mountain."

Just then they came to another curve in their path, and saw a bright light ahead. It looked to the children just like daylight;

so they ran along and soon passed through a low arch and came out into —

Well! the scene before them was so strange that it nearly took away their breath, and they stood perfectly still and stared as hard as their big eyes could possibly stare.

Chapter 3

Sugar-Loaf City

S ugar-Loaf Mountain was hollow inside, for the children stood facing a great dome that rose so far above their heads that it seemed almost as high as the sky. And underneath this dome lay spread out the loveliest city imaginable. There were streets of houses, and buildings with round domes, and slender, delicate spires reaching far up into the air, and turrets beautifully ornamented with carvings. And all these were white as the driven snow and sparkling in every part like millions of diamonds — for all were built of pure loaf-sugar! The pavements of the streets were also loaf-sugar, and the trees and bushes and flowers were likewise sugar; but these last were not all white, because all sugar is not white, and they showed many bright colors of red sugar and blue sugar and yellow, purple and green sugar, all contrasting most prettily with the sparkling white buildings and the great white dome over-head.

This alone might well astonish the eyes of children from the outside world, but it was by no means all that Twinkle and Chubbins beheld in that first curious look at Sugar-Loaf City. For the city was inhabited by many people — men, women and children — who walked along the streets just as briskly as we do; only all were made of sugar. There were several different kinds of these sugar people. Some, who strutted proudly along, were evidently of pure loaf-sugar, and these were of a most respectable appearance. Others seemed to be made of a light brown sugar, and were more humble in their manners and seemed to hurry along as if they had business to attend to. Then there were some of sugar so dark in color that Twinkle suspected it was maple-sugar, and these folks seemed of less account than any of the others, being servants, drivers of carriages, and beggars and idlers.

Carts and carriages moved along the streets, and were mostly made of brown sugar. The horses that drew them were either pressed sugar or maple-sugar. In fact, everything that existed in this wonderful city was made of some kind of sugar.

Where the light, which made all this place so bright and beautiful, came from, Twinkle could not imagine. There was no sun, nor were there any electric lights that could be seen; but it was fully as bright as day and everything showed with great plainness.

While the children, who stood just inside the archway through which they had entered, were looking at the wonders of Sugar-Loaf City, a file of sugar soldiers suddenly came around a corner at a swift trot.

"Halt!" cried the Captain. He wore a red sugar jacket and a red sugar cap, and the soldiers were dressed in the same manner as their Captain, but without the officer's yellow sugar shoulder-straps. At the command, the sugar soldiers came to a stop, and all pointed their sugar muskets at Twinkle and Chubbins.

"Surrender!" said the Captain to them. "Surrender, or I'll — I'll — "

He hesitated.

"What will you do?" said Twinkle.

"I don't know what, but something very dreadful, replied the Captain. "But of course you'll surrender."

"I suppose we'll have to," answered the girl.

"Surrender!" said the Captain

"That's right. I'll just take you to the king, and let him decide what to do," he added pleasantly.

So the soldiers surrounded the two children, shouldered arms, and marched away down the street, Twinkle and Chubbins walking slowly, so the candy folks would not have to run; for the tallest soldiers were only as high as their shoulders.

"This is a great event," remarked the Captain, as he walked beside them with as much dignity as he could muster. "It was really good of you to come and be arrested, for I haven't had any excitement in a long time. The people here are such good sugar that they seldom do anything wrong."

Chapter 4

To the King's Palace

"What, allow me to ask, is your grade of sugar?" inquired the Captain, with much politeness. "You do not seem to be the best loaf, but I suppose that of course you are solid."

"Solid what?" asked Chubbins.

"Solid sugar," replied the Captain.

"We're not sugar at all," explained Twinkle. "We're just meat."

"Meat! And what is that?"

"Haven't you any meat in your city?"

"No," he replied, shaking his head.

"Well, I can't explain exactly what meat is," she said; "but it isn't sugar, anyway."

At this the Captain looked solemn.

"It isn't any of my business, after all," he told them. "The king must decide about you, for that's *his* business. But since you are not made of sugar you must excuse me if I decline to converse with you any longer. It is beneath my dignity."

"Oh, that's all right," said Twinkle.

"Where we came from," said Chubbins, "meat costs more a pound than sugar does; so I guess we're just as good as you are."

But the Captain made no reply to this statement, and before

long they stopped in front of a big sugar building, while a crowd of sugar people quickly gathered.

"Stand back!" cried the Captain, and the sugar soldiers formed a row between the children and the sugar citizens, and kept the crowd from getting too near. Then the Captain led Twinkle and Chubbins through a high sugar gateway and up a broad sugar walk to the entrance of the building.

"Must be the king's castle," said Chubbins.

"The king's palace," corrected the Captain, stiffly.

"What's the difference?" asked Twinkle.

But the sugar officer did not care to explain.

Brown sugar servants in plum-colored sugar coats stood at the entrance to the palace, and their eyes stuck out like lozenges from their sugar faces when they saw the strangers the Captain was escorting.

But every one bowed low, and stood aside for them to pass, and they walked through beautiful halls and reception rooms where the sugar was cut into panels and scrolls and carved to represent all kinds of fruit and flowers.

"Isn't it sweet!" said Twinkle.

"Sure it is," answered Chubbins.

And now they were ushered into a magnificent room, where a stout little sugar man was sitting near the window playing upon a fiddle, while a group of sugar men and women stood before him in respectful attitudes and listened to the music.

Twinkle knew at once that the fiddler was the king, because he had a sugar crown upon his head. His Majesty was made of very white and sparkling cut loaf-sugar, and his clothing was formed of the same pure material. The only color about him was the pink sugar in his cheeks and the brown sugar in his eyes. His fiddle was also of white sugar, and the strings were of spun sugar and had an excellent tone.

When the king saw the strange children enter the room he jumped up and exclaimed:

"Bless my beets! What have we here?"

"Mortals, Most Granular and Solidified Majesty," answered the Captain, bowing so low that his forehead touched the floor. "They came in by the ancient tunnel."

"Well, I declare," said the king. "I thought that tunnel had been stopped up for good and all."

"The stone above the door slipped," said Twinkle, "so we came down to see what we could find."

"You must never do it again," said his Majesty, sternly. "This is our own kingdom, a peaceful and retired nation of extra refined and substantial citizens, and we don't wish to mix with mortals, or any other folks."

"We'll go back, pretty soon," said Twinkle.

"Now, that's very nice of you," declared the king, "and I appreciate your kindness. Are you extra refined, my dear?"

"I hope so," said the girl, a little doubtfully.

"Then there's no harm in our being friendly while you're here. And as you've promised to go back to your own world soon, I have no objection to showing you around the town. You'd like to see how we live, wouldn't you?"

"Very much," said Twinkle.

"Order my chariot, Captain Brittle," said his Majesty; and the Captain again made one of his lowly bows and strutted from the room to execute the command.

The king now introduced Chubbins and Twinkle to the sugar ladies and gentlemen who were present, and all of them treated the children very respectfully.

Chapter 5

Princess Sakareen

"Say, play us a tune," said Chubbins to the king. His Majesty didn't seem to like being addressed so bluntly, but he was very fond of playing the fiddle, so he graciously obeyed the request and played a pretty and pathetic ballad upon the spun sugar strings. Then, begging to be excused for a few minutes while the chariot was being made ready, the king left them and went into another room.

This gave the children a chance to talk freely with the sugar people, and Chubbins said to one man, who looked very smooth on the outside:

"I s'pose you're one of the big men of this place, aren't you?"

The man looked frightened for a moment, and then took the boy's arm and led him into a corner of the room.

"You ask me an embarrassing question," he whispered, looking around to make sure that no one overheard. "Although I pose as one of the nobility, I am, as a matter of fact, a great fraud!"

"How's that? asked Chubbins.

"Have you noticed how smooth I am?" inquired the sugar man.

"Yes," replied the boy. "Why is it?"

"Why, I'm frosted, that's the reason. No one here suspects it, and I'm considered very respectable; but the truth is, I'm just coated over with frosting, and not solid sugar at all."

"What's inside you?" asked Chubbins.

"That," answered the man, "I do not know. I've never dared to find out. For if I broke my frosting to see what I'm stuffed with, every one else would see too, and I would be disgraced and ruined."

"Perhaps you're cake," suggested the boy.

"Perhaps so," answered the man, sadly. "Please keep my secret, for only those who are solid loaf-sugar are of any account in this country, and at present I am received in the best society, as you see."

"Oh, I won't tell," said Chubbins.

During this time Twinkle had been talking with a sugar lady, in another part of the room. This lady seemed to be of the purest loaf-sugar, for she sparkled most beautifully, and Twinkle thought she was quite the prettiest person to look at that she had yet seen.

"Are you related to the king?" she asked.

"No, indeed," answered the sugar lady, "although I'm considered one of the very highest quality. But I'll tell you a secret, my dear." She took Twinkle's hand and led her across to a sugar sofa, where they both sat down.

"No one," resumed the sugar lady, "has ever suspected the truth; but I'm only a sham, and it worries me dreadfully."

"I don't understand what you mean," said Twinkle. "Your sugar seems as pure and sparkling as that of the king."

"Things are not always what they seem," sighed the sugar lady. "What you see of me, on the outside, is all right; but the fact is, *I'm hollow!*"

"Dear me!" exclaimed Twinkle, in surprise. "How do you know it?"

"I can feel it," answered the lady, impressively. "If you weighed me you'd find I'm not as heavy as the solid ones, and for a long time I've realized the bitter truth that I'm hollow. It makes me very unhappy, but I don't dare confide my secret to anyone here, because it would disgrace me forever."

"I wouldn't worry," said the child. "They'll never know the difference."

"Not unless I should break," replied the sugar lady. "But if that happened, all the world could see that I'm hollow, and instead of being welcomed in good society I'd become an outcast. It's even more respectable to be made of brown sugar, than to be hollow; don't you think so?"

"I'm a stranger here," said Twinkle; "so I can't judge. But if I were you, I wouldn't worry unless I got broke; and you may be wrong, after all, and as sound as a brick!"

Chapter 6

The Royal Chariot

J ust then the king came back to the room and said:

"The chariot is at the door; and, as there are three seats, I'll take Lord Cloy and Princess Sakareen with us."

So the children followed the king to the door of the palace, where stood a beautiful white and yellow sugar chariot, drawn by six handsome sugar horses with spun sugar tails and manes, and driven by a brown sugar coachman in a blue sugar livery.

The king got in first, and the others followed. Then the children discovered that Lord Cloy was the frosted man and Princess Sakareen was the sugar lady who had told Twinkle that she was hollow.

There was quite a crowd of sugar people at the gates to watch the departure of the royal party, and a few soldiers and policemen were also present to keep order. Twinkle sat beside the king, and Chubbins sat on the same seat with the Princess Sakareen, while Lord Cloy was obliged to sit with the coachman. When all were ready the driver cracked a sugar whip (but didn't break it), and away the chariot dashed over a road paved with blocks of cut loaf-sugar.

The air was cool and pleasant, but there was a sweet smell to the breeze that was peculiar to this strange country. Sugar birds flew here and there, singing sweet songs, and a few sugar dogs ran out to bark at the king's chariot as it whirled along.

"Haven't you any automobiles in your country?" asked the girl.

"No," answered the king. "Anything that requires heat to make it go is avoided here, because heat would melt us and ruin our bodies in a few minutes. Automobiles would be dangerous in Sugar-Loaf City."

"They're dangerous enough anywhere," she said. "What do you feed to your horses?"

"They eat a fine quality of barley-sugar that grows in our fields," answered the king. "You'll see it presently, for we will drive out to my country villa, which is near the edge of the dome, opposite to where you came in."

First, however, they rode all about the city, and the king pointed out the public buildings, and the theaters, and the churches, and a number of small but pretty public parks. And there was a high tower near the center that rose half-way to the dome, it was so tall.

"Aren't you afraid the roof will cave in some time, and ruin your city?" Twinkle asked the king.

"Oh, no," he answered. "We never think of such a thing. Isn't there a dome over the place where you live?"

"Yes," said Twinkle; "but it's the sky."

"Do you ever fear it will cave in?" inquired the king.

"No, indeed!" she replied, with a laugh at the idea.

"Well, it's the same way with us," returned his Majesty. "Domes are the strongest things in all the world."

Chapter 7

Twinkle Gets Thirsty

After they had seen the sights of the city the carriage turned into a broad highway that led into the country, and soon they began to pass fields of sugar corn and gardens of sugar cabbages and sugar beets and sugar potatoes. There were also orchards of sugar plums and sugar apples and vineyards of sugar grapes. All the trees were sugar, and even the grass was sugar, while sugar grasshoppers hopped about in it. Indeed, Chubbins decided that not a speck of anything beneath the dome of Sugar-Loaf Mountain was anything but pure sugar — unless the inside of the frosted man proved to be of a different material.

By and by they reached a pretty villa, where they all left the carriage and followed the sugar king into the sugar house. Refreshments had been ordered in advance, over the sugar telephone, so that the dining table was already laid and all they had to do was to sit in the pretty sugar chairs and be waited upon by maple-sugar attendants.

There were sandwiches and salads and fruits and many other sugar things to eat, served on sugar plates; and the children found that some were flavored with wintergreen and raspberry and lemon, so that they were almost as good as candies. At each plate was a glass made of crystal sugar and filled with thick sugar syrup, and this seemed to be the only thing to drink. After eating so much sugar the children naturally became thirsty, and when the king asked Twinkle if she would like anything else she answered promptly:

"Yes, I'd like a drink of water."

At once a murmur of horror arose form the sugar people present, and the king pushed back his chair as if greatly disturbed.

"Water!" he exclaimed, in amazement.

"Sure," replied Chubbins. "I want some, too. We're thirsty."

The king shuddered.

"Nothing in the world," said he gravely, "is so dangerous as water. It melts sugar in no time, and to drink it would destroy you instantly."

"We're not made of sugar," said Twinkle. "In our country we drink all the water we want."

"It may be true," returned the king; "but I am thankful to say there is no drop of water in all this favored country. But we have syrup, which is much better for your health. It fills up the spaces inside you, and hardens and makes you solid."

"It makes me thirstier than ever," said the girl. "But if you have no water we must try to get along until we get home again."

When the luncheon was over, they entered the carriage again and were driven back towards the city. On the way the six sugar horses became restless, and pranced around in so lively a manner that the sugar coachman could scarcely hold them in. And when they had nearly reached the palace a part of the harness broke, and without warning all six horses dashed madly away. The chariot smashed against a high wall of sugar and broke into many pieces, the sugar people, as well as Twinkle and Chubbins, being thrown out and scattered in all directions.

The little girl was not at all hurt, nor was Chubbins, who landed on top the wall and had to climb down again. But the king had broken one of the points off his crown, and sat upon

The Princess' leg had broken

the ground gazing sorrowfully at his wrecked chariot. And Lord Cloy, the frosted man, had smashed one of his feet, and everybody could now see that underneath the frosting was a material very like marshmallow — a discovery that was sure to condemn him as unfit for the society of the solid sugar-loaf aristocracy of the country.

But perhaps the most serious accident of all had befallen Princess Sakareen, whose left leg had broken short off at the knee. Twinkle ran up to her as soon as she could, and found the Princess smiling happily and gazing at the part of the broken leg which she had picked up.

"See here, Twinkle," she cried; "it's as solid as the king himself! I'm not hollow at all. It was only my imagination."

"I'm glad of that," answered Twinkle; "but what will you do with a broken leg?"

"Oh, that's easily mended," said the Princess. "All I must do is to put a little syrup on the broken parts, and stick them together, and then sit in the breeze until it hardens. I'll be all right in an hour from now."

It pleased Twinkle to hear this, for she liked the pretty sugar princess.

Chapter 8

After the Runaway

"Now the king came up to them, saying: "I hope you are not injured."

"We are all right," said Twinkle; "but I'm getting dreadful thirsty, so if your Majesty has no objection I guess we'll go home."

"No objection at all," answered the king.

Chubbins had been calmly filling his pockets with broken spokes and other bits of the wrecked chariot; but feeling nearly as thirsty as Twinkle, he was glad to learn they were about to start for home.

They exchanged good-byes with all their sugar friends, and thanked the sugar king for his royal entertainment. Then Captain Brittle and his soldiers escorted the children to the archway through which they had entered Sugar-Loaf City.

They had little trouble in going back, although the tunnel was so dark in places that they had to feel their way. But finally daylight could be seen ahead, and a few minutes later they scrambled up the stone steps and squeezed through the little doorway.

There was their basket, just as they had left it, and the afternoon sun was shining softly over the familiar worldly landscape, which they were both rejoiced to see again.

Chubbins closed the iron door, and as soon as he did so the bolts shot into place, locking it securely.

"Where's the key?" asked Twinkle.

"I put it into my pocket," said Chubbins, "but it must have dropped out when I tumbled from the king's chariot."

"That's too bad," said Twinkle; "for now no one can ever get to the sugar city again. The door is locked, and the key is on the other side."

"Never mind," said the boy. "We've seen the inside of Sugar-Loaf Mountain once, and that'll do us all our lives. Come on, Twink. Let's go home and get a drink!"

Policeman Bluejay

Chapter 1

Little Ones in Trouble

"Seems to me, Chub," said Twinkle, "that we're lost."

"Seems to me, Twink," said Chubbins, "that it isn't *we* that's lost. It's the path."

"It was here a minute ago," declared Twinkle.

"But it isn't here now," replied the boy.

"That's true," said the girl.

It really *was* queer. They had followed the straight path into the great forest, and had only stopped for a moment to sit down and rest, with the basket between them and their backs to a big tree. Twinkle winked just twice, because she usually took a nap in the afternoon, and Chubbins merely closed his eyes a second to find out if he could see that long streak of sunshine through his pink eyelids. Yet during this second, which happened while Twinkle was winking, the path had run away and left them without any guide or any notion which way they ought to go.

Another strange thing was that when they jumped up to look around them the nearest trees began sliding away, in a circle, leaving the little girl and boy in a clear space. And the trees continued moving back and back, farther and farther, until all their trunks were jammed tight together, and not even a mouse could have crept between them. They made a solid ring around Twinkle and Chubbins, who stood looking at this transformation with wondering eyes.

Little ones in trouble

"It's a trap," said Chubbins; "and we're in it."

"It looks that way," replied Twinkle, thoughtfully. "Isn't it lucky, Chub, we have the basket with us? If it wasn't for that, we might starve to death in our prison."

"Oh, well," replied the little fellow, "the basket won't last long. There's plenty of starve in the bottom of it, Twinkle, any way you can fix it."

"That's so; unless we can get out. Whatever do you suppose made the trees behave that way, Chubbins?"

"Don't know," said the boy.

Just then a queer creature dropped from a tree into the ring and began moving slowly toward them. It was flat in shape, like a big turtle; only it hadn't a turtle's hard shell. Instead, its body was covered with sharp prickers, like rose thorns, and it had two small red eyes that looked cruel and wicked. The children could not see how many legs it had, but they must have been very short, because the creature moved so slowly over the ground.

When it had drawn near to them it said, in a pleading tone that sounded soft and rather musical:

"Little girl, pick me up in your arms, and pet me!"

Twinkle shrank back.

"My! I couldn't *think* of doing such a thing," she answered.

Then the creature said:

"Little boy, please pick me up in your arms, and pet me!"

"Go 'way!" shouted Chubbins. "I wouldn't touch you for any-thing."

The creature turned its red eyes first upon one and then upon the other.

"Listen, my dears," it continued; "I was once a beautiful maiden, but a cruel tuxix transformed me into this awful shape, and so must I remain until some child willingly takes me in its arms and pets me. Then, and not till then, will I be restored to my proper form."

"Don't believe it! Don't believe it!" cried a high, clear voice, and both the boy and the girl looked quickly around to see who had spoken. But no one besides themselves was in sight, and they only noticed a thick branch of one of the trees slightly swaying its leaves.

"What is a tuxix?" asked Twinkle, who was beginning to feel sorry for the poor creature.

"It is a magician, a sorcerer, a wizard, and a witch all rolled into one," was the answer; "and you can imagine what a dreadful thing that would be."

"Be careful!" cried the clear voice, again. "It is the tuxix herself who is talking to you. Don't believe a word you hear!"

At this the red eyes of the creature flashed fire with anger, and it tried to turn its clumsy body around to find the speaker. Twinkle and Chubbins looked too, but only heard a flutter and a mocking laugh coming from the trees.

"If I get my eye on that bird, it will never speak again," exclaimed the creature, in a voice of fury very different from the sweet tones it had at first used; and perhaps it was this fact that induced the children to believe the warning was from a friend, and they would do well to heed it.

"Whether you are the tuxix or not," said Twinkle, "I never will touch you. You may be sure of that."

"Nor I," declared Chubbins, stoutly, as he came closer to the girl and grasped her hand in his own.

At this the horrid thing bristled all its sharp prickers in anger, and said:

"Then, if I cannot conquer you in one way, I will in another. Go, both of you, and join the bird that warned you, and live in the air and the trees until you repent your stubbornness and promise to become my slaves. The tuxix has spoken, and her magical powers are at work. Go!"

In an instant Twinkle saw Chubbins shoot through the air and disappear among the leaves of one of the tall trees. As he went he seemed to grow very small, and to change in shape.

"Wait!" she cried. "I'm coming, too!"

She was afraid of losing Chubbins, so she flew after him, feeling rather queer herself, and a moment after was safe in the tall tree, clinging with her toes to a branch and looking in amazement at the boy who sat beside her.

Chubbins had been transformed into a pretty little bird — all, that is, except his head, which was Chubbins' own head reduced in size to fit the bird body. It still had upon it the straw hat, which had also grown small in size, and the sight that met Twinkle's eyes was so funny that she laughed merrily, and her laugh was like the sweet warbling of a skylark.

Chubbins looked at her and saw almost what she saw; for Twinkle was a bird too, except for her head, with its checked sunbonnet, which had grown small enough to fit the pretty, glossy-feathered body of a lark.

Both of them had to cling fast to the branch with their toes, for their arms and hands were now wings. The toes were long and sharp pointed, so that they could be used in the place of fingers.

"My!" exclaimed Twinkle; "you're a queer sight, Chubbins!"

"So are you," answered the boy. "That mean old thing must have 'witched us."

"Yes, we're 'chanted," said Twinkle. "And now, what are we going to do about it? We can't go home, for our folks would be scared nearly into fits. And we don't know the way home, either."

"That's so," said Chubbins, fluttering his little wings to keep from falling, for he had nearly lost his balance.

"So what shall we do?" she continued.

"Why, fly around and be gay and happy," said a clear and merry voice beside them. "That's what birds are expected to do!"

Chapter 2

The Forest Guardian

Twinkle and Chubbins twisted their heads around on their little feathered necks and saw perched beside them a big bird of a most beautiful blue color. At first they were a bit frightened, for the newcomer seemed of a giant size beside their little lark bodies, and he was, moreover, quite fierce in appearance, having a crest of feathers that came to a point above his head, and a strong beak and sharp talons. But Twinkle looked full into the shrewd, bright eye, and found it good humored and twinkling; so she plucked up courage and asked:

"Were you speaking to us?"

"Very likely," replied the blue bird, in a cheerful tone. "There's no one else around to speak to."

"And was it you who warned us against that dreadful creature below in the forest?" she continued.

"It was."

"Then," said Twinkle, "we are very much obliged to you."

"Don't mention it," said the other. "I'm the forest policeman — Policeman Bluejay, you know — and it's my duty to look after everyone who is in trouble."

"We're in trouble, all right," said Chubbins, sorrowfully.

"Well, it might have been worse," remarked Policeman Bluejay, making a chuckling sound in his throat that Twinkle thought was meant for a laugh. "If you had ever touched the old tuxix she would have transformed you into toads or lizards. That is an old trick of hers, to get children into her power and then change them into things as loathsome as herself."

"I wouldn't have touched her, anyhow," said Twinkle.

"Nor I!" cried Chubbins, in his shrill, bird-like voice. "She wasn't nice."

"Still, it was good of you to warn us," Twinkle added, sweetly.

The Bluejay looked upon the fluttering little things with kind approval. Then he laughed outright.

"What has happened to your heads?" he asked.

"Nothing, 'cept they're smaller," replied Chubbins.

"But birds shouldn't have human heads," retorted the bluejay. "I suppose the old tuxix did that so the birds would not admit you into their society, for you are neither all bird nor all human. But never mind; I'll explain your case, and you may be sure all the birds of the forest will be kind to you."

"Must we stay like this always?" asked Twinkle, anxiously.

"I really can't say," answered the policeman. "There is said to be a way to break every enchantment, if one knows what it is. The trouble in these cases is to discover what the charm may be that will restore you to your natural shapes. But just now you must make up your minds to live in our forest for a time, and to be as happy as you can under the circumstances."

"Well, we'll try," said Chubbins, with a sigh.

"That's right," exclaimed Policeman Bluejay, nodding his crest in approval. "The first thing you must have is a house; so, if you will fly with me, I will try to find you one."

"I — I'm afraid!" said Twinkle, nervously.

"The larks," declared the bluejay, "are almost the strongest and best flyers we have. You two children have now become sky-larks, and may soar so high in the air that you can scarcely see the earth below you. For that reason you need have no fear whatever. Be bold and brave, and all will be well."

He spoke in such a kindly and confident voice that both Twinkle and Chubbins gained courage; and when the policeman added: "Come on!" and flew straight as an arrow into the air above the tree-tops, the two little skylarks with their girl and boy heads followed swiftly after him, and had no trouble in going just as fast as their conductor.

It was quite a pleasant and interesting experience, to dart through the air and be in no danger of falling. When they rested on their outstretched wings they floated as lightly as bubbles, and soon a joyous thrill took possession of them and they began to understand why it is that the free, wild birds are always so happy in their native state.

The forest was everywhere under them, for it was of vast extent. Presently the bluejay swooped downward and alighted near the top of a tall maple tree that had many thick branches.

In a second Twinkle and Chubbins were beside him, their little hearts beating fast in their glossy bosoms from the excitement of their rapid flight. Just in front of them, firmly fastened to a crotch of a limb, was a neatly built nest of a gray color, lined inside with some soft substance that was as smooth as satin.

"Here," said their thoughtful friend, "is the nest that Niddie Thrush and Daisy Thrush built for themselves a year ago. They have now gone to live in a wood across the big river, so you are welcome to their old home. It is almost as good as new, and there is no rent to pay."

"It's awfully small!" said Chubbins.

"Chut-Chut!" twittered Policeman Bluejay. "Remember you are not children now, but skylarks, and that this is a thrush's nest. Try it, and you are sure to find it will fit you exactly."

So Twinkle and Chubbins flew into the "house" and nestled their bodies against its soft lining and found that their friend was right. When they were cuddled together, with their slender legs tucked into the feathers of their breasts, they just filled the nest to the brim, and no more room was necessary.

"Now, I'll mark the nest for you, so that everyone will know you claim it," said the policeman; and with his bill he pecked a row of small dots in the bark of the limb, just beside the nest. "I hope you will be very happy here, and this afternoon I will bring some friends to meet you. So now good-bye until I see you again."

"Wait!" cried Chubbins. "What are we going to eat?"

"Eat!" answered the bluejay, as if surprised. "Why, you may feast upon all the good things the forest offers — grubs, beetles, worms, and butterfly-eggs."

"Ugh!" gasped Chubbins. "It makes me sick to just think of it."

"What!"

"You see," said Twinkle, "we are not *all* bird, Mr. Bluejay, as you are; and that makes a big difference. We have no bills to pick up the things that birds like to eat, and we do not care for the same sort of food either."

"What *do* you care for?" asked the policeman, in a puzzled voice.

"Why, cake and sandwiches, and pickles, and cheese, such as we had in our basket. We couldn't eat any *live* things, you see, because we are not used to it."

The bluejay became thoughtful.

"I understand your objection," he said, "and perhaps you are right, not having good bird sense because the brains in your heads are still human brains. Let me see: what can I do to help you?"

The children did not speak, but watched him anxiously.

"Where did you leave your basket?" he finally asked.

"In the place where the old witch 'chanted us."

"Then," said the officer of the forest, "I must try to get it for you."

"It is too big and heavy for a bird to carry," suggested Twinkle.

"Sure enough. Of course. That's a fact." He turned his crested head upward, trying to think of a way, and saw a black speck moving across the sky.

"Wait a minute! I'll be back," he called, and darted upward like a flash.

The children watched him mount into the sky toward the black speck, and heard his voice crying out in sharp, quick notes. And before long Policeman Bluejay attracted the other bird's attention, causing it to pause in its flight and sink slowly downward until the two drew close together.

Then it was seen that the other bird was a great eagle, strong and sharp-eyed, and with broad wings that spread at least six feet from tip to tip.

"Good day, friend eagle," said the bluejay; "I hope you are in no hurry, for I want to ask you to do me a great favor."

"What is it?" asked the eagle, in a big, deep voice.

"Please go to a part of the forest with me and carry a basket to some friends of mine. I'll show you the way. It is too heavy for me to lift, but with your great strength you can do it easily."

"It will give me pleasure to so favor you," replied the eagle, politely; so Policeman Bluejay led the way and the eagle followed with such mighty strokes of its wings that the air was sent whirling in little eddies behind him, as the water is churned by a steamer's paddles.

It was not very long before they reached the clearing in the forest. The horrid tuxix had wriggled her evil body away, to soothe her disappointment by some other wicked act; but the basket stood as the children had left it.

The eagle seized the handle in his stout beak and found it

was no trouble at all for him to fly into the air and carry the basket with him.

"This way, please — this way!" chirped the bluejay; and the eagle bore the precious burden safely to the maple tree, and hung it upon a limb just above the nest.

As he approached he made such a fierce fluttering that Twinkle and Chubbins were dreadfully scared and flew out of their nest, hopping from limb to limb until they were well out of the monstrous bird's way. But when they saw the basket, and realized the eagle's kindly act, they flew toward him and thanked him very earnestly for his assistance.

"Goodness me!" exclaimed the eagle, turning his head first on one side and then on the other, that both his bright eyes might observe the child-larks; "what curious creatures have you here, my good policeman?"

"Why, it is another trick of old Hautau, the tuxix. She found two children in the forest and enchanted them. She wanted to make them toads, but they wouldn't touch her, so she couldn't. Then she got herself into a fine range and made the little dears half birds and half children, as you see them. I was in a tree near by, and saw the whole thing. Because I was sorry for the innocent victims I befriended them, and as this basket belongs to them I have asked you to fetch it to their nest."

"I am glad to be of service," replied the eagle. "If ever you need me, and I am anywhere around," he continued, addressing the larks, "just call me, and I will come at once."

"Thank you," said Twinkle, gratefully.

"We're much obliged," added Chubbins.

Then the eagle flew away, and when he was gone Policeman Bluejay also bade them good-bye.

"I'll be back this afternoon, without fail," he said. "Just now I must go and look over the forest, and make sure none of the birds have been in mischief during my absence. Do not go very far from your nest, for a time, or you may get lost. The forest is a big place; but when you are more used to it and to your new condition you can be more bold in venturing abroad."

"We won't leave this tree," promised Twinkle, in an earnest voice.

And Chubbins chimed in with, "That's right; we won't leave this tree until you come back."

"Good-bye," said the policeman.

"Good-bye," responded Twinkle and Chubbins.

So the bluejay darted away and was soon lost to sight, and Twinkle and Chubbins were left alone to seriously consider the great misfortune that had overtaken them.

Chapter 3

The Child-Larks

"Folks will be worried about us, Twink," said Chubbins.

" 'Course they will," Twinkle replied. "They'll wonder what has become of us, and try to find us."

"But they won't look in the tree-tops."

"No."

"Nor think to ask the birds where we are."

"Why should they?" enquired Twinkle. "They can't talk to the birds, Chub."

"Why not? We talk to them, don't we? And they talk to us. At least, the p'liceman and the eagle did."

"That's true," answered Twinkle, "and I don't understand it a bit. I must ask Mr. Bluejay to 'splain it to us."

"What's the use of a p'liceman in the forest?" asked Chubbins, after a moment's thought.

"I suppose," she replied, "that he has to keep the birds from being naughty. Some birds are just awful mischiefs, Chub. There's the magpies, you know, that steal; and the crows that fight; and the jackdaws that are saucy, and lots of others that get into trouble. Seems to me P'liceman Bluejay's a pretty busy bird, if he looks after things as he ought."

"Prob'ly he's got his hands full," said Chubbins.

"Not that; for he hasn't any hands, any more than we have.

Perhaps you ought to say he's got his wings full," suggested Twinkle.

"That reminds me I'm hungry," chirped the boy-lark.

"Well, we've got the basket," she replied.

"But how can we eat cake and things, witched up as we are?"

"Haven't we mouths and teeth, just the same as ever?"

"Yes, but we haven't any hands, and there's a cloth tied over the top of the basket."

"Dear me!" exclaimed Twinkle; "I hadn't thought of that."

They flew together to the basket and perched upon the edge of it. It seemed astonishingly big to them, now that they were so small; but Chubbins remarked that this fact was a pleasant one, for instead of eating all the good things the basket contained at one meal, as they had at first intended, it would furnish them with food for many days to come.

But how to get into the basket was the thing to be considered just now. They fluttered around on every side of it, and finally found a small place where the cloth was loose. In a minute Chubbins began clawing at it with his little feet, and Twinkle helped him; so that gradually they managed to pull the cloth away far enough for one of them to crawl through the opening. Then the other followed, and because the big basket was not quite full there was exactly room for them to stand underneath the cloth and walk around on top of a row of cookies that lay next to a row of sandwiches.

The cookies seemed enormous. One was lying flat, and Chubbins declared it seemed as big around as the dining-table at home.

"All the better for us," said Twinkle, bending her head down to nibble at the edge of the cookie.

"If we're going to be birds," said Chubbins, who was also busily eating as best he could, "we ought to be reg'lar birds, and have bills to peck with. This being half one thing and half another doesn't suit me at all."

"The witch wasn't trying to suit us," replied Twinkle; "she was trying to get us into trouble."

"Well, she did it, all right," he said.

It was not so hard to eat as they had feared, for their slender necks enabled them to bend their heads low. Chubbins' hat fell off, a minute later, and he wondered how he was going to get it on his head again.

"Can't you stand on one foot, and use the other foot like a hand?" asked Twinkle.

"I don't know," he said.

"The storks stand on one leg," continued the girl. "I've seen 'em in pictures."

So Chubbins tried it, and found he could balance his little body on one leg very nicely. For if he toppled either way he had but to spread his wings and tail feathers and so keep himself from falling. He picked up his hat with the claws of his other foot and managed to put it on by ducking his head.

This gave the boy-lark a new idea. He broke off a piece of the cookie and held it in his claw while he ate it; and seeing his success Twinkle followed his example, and after a few attempts found she could eat very comfortably in that way.

Having had their luncheon — and it amazed Chubbins to see how very little was required to satisfy their hunger — the bird-children crept out of the basket and flew down to the twig beside their nest.

"Hello!" cried a strange voice. "Newcomers, eh?"

They were so startled that they fluttered a moment to keep from tumbling off the limb. Then Twinkle saw a furry red head sticking out of a small hollow in the trunk of the tree. The head had two round black eyes, an inquisitive nose, a wide mouth with sharp teeth and whiskers like those of a cat. It seemed as big as the moon to the shy little child-larks, until it occurred to the girl that the strange creature must be a squirrel.

"You — you scared us!" she said, timidly.

"You scared *me*, at first," returned the squirrel, in a comic tone. "Dear me! how came you birds to have children's heads?"

"That isn't the way to put it," remarked Chubbins, staring back into the eyes of the squirrel. "You should ask how we children happened to have birds' bodies."

"Very well; put the conundrum that way, if you like," said the squirrel. "What is the answer?"

"We are enchanted," replied Twinkle.

"Ah. The tuxix?"

"Yes. We were caught in the forest, and she bewitched us."

"That is too bad," said their new acquaintance. "She is a very wicked old creature, for a fact, and loves to get folks into trouble. Are you going to live here?"

"Yes," answered the girl. "Policeman Bluejay gave us this nest."

"Then it's all right; for Policeman Bluejay rules the feathered tribes of this forest about as he likes. Have you seen him in full uniform yet?"

"No," they replied, "unless his feathers are his uniform."

"Well, he's too proud of his office to be satisfied with feathers, I can tell you. When some folks get a little authority they want all the world to know about it, and a bold uniform covers many a faint heart. But as I'm your nearest neighbor I'll introduce myself. My name's Wisk."

"My name is Twinkle."

"And mine's Chubbins."

"Pleased to make your acquaintance," said the squirrel, nodding. "I live in the second flat."

"How's that?" asked the boy.

"Why, the second hollow, you know. There's a 'possum living

in the hollow down below, who is carrying four babies around in her pocket; and Mrs. Hootaway, the gray owl, lives in the hollow above — the one you can see far over your heads. So I'm the second flat tenant."

"I see," said Twinkle.

"Early in the morning the 'possum comes growling home to go to bed; late at night the owl hoots and keeps folks awake; but I'm very quiet and well behaved, and you'll find me a good neighbor," continued Wisk.

"I'm sure of that," said Chubbins.

As if to prove his friendship the squirrel now darted out of the hollow and sat upon a limb beside the children, holding his bushy tail straight up so that it stood above his head like a big plume in a soldier's helmet.

"Are you hungry?" asked the girl.

"Not very. I cannot get much food until the nuts are ripe, you know, and my last winter's supply was gone long ago. But I manage to find some bits to eat, here and there."

"Do you like cookies?" she asked.

"I really do not know," answered Wisk. "Where do they grow?"

"In baskets. I'll get you a piece, and you can try it."

So Twinkle flew up and crept into her basket again, quickly returning with a bit of cookie in her claw. It was not much more than a crumb, but nevertheless it was all that she could carry.

The squirrel seized the morsel in his paws, examined it gravely, and then took a nibble. An instant later it was gone.

"That is very good, indeed!" he declared. "Where do these baskets of cookies grow?"

"They don't grow anywhere," replied Twinkle, with a laugh. "The baskets come from the grocery store, and my mama makes the cookies."

"Oh; they're human food, then."

"Yes; would you like some more?"

"Not just now," said Wisk. " I don't want to rob you, and it is foolish to eat more than one needs, just because the food tastes good. But if I get very hungry, perhaps I'll ask you for another bite."

"Do," said the girl. "You are welcome to what we have, as long as it lasts."

"That is very kind of you," returned the squirrel.

They sat and talked for an hour, and Wisk told them stories of the forest, and of the many queer animals and birds that lived there. It was all very interesting to the children, and they listened eagerly until they heard a rushing sound in the air that sent Wisk scurrying back into his hole.

Chapter 4

An Afternoon Reception

T winkle and Chubbins stretched their little necks to see what was coming, and a moment later beheld one of the most gorgeous sights the forest affords — a procession of all the bright-hued birds that live among the trees or seek them for shelter.

They flew in pairs, one after the other, and at the head of the procession was their good friend Policeman Bluejay, wearing a policeman's helmet upon his head and having a policeman's club tucked underneath his left wing. The helmet was black and glossy and had a big number "1" on the front of it, and a strap that passed under the wearer's bill and held it firmly in place. The club was fastened around the policeman's wing with a cord, so that it could not get away when he was flying.

The birds were of many sizes and of various colorings. Some were much larger than the bluejay, but none seemed so proud or masterful, and all deferred meekly to the commands of the acknowledged guardian of the forest.

One by one the pretty creatures alighted upon the limbs of the tree, and the first thing they all did was to arrange their feathers properly after their rapid flight. Then the bluejay, who sat next to the child-larks, proceeded to introduce the guests he had brought to call upon the newest inhabitants of his domain.

"This is Mr. and Mrs. Robin Redbreast, one of our most aristocratic families," said he, swinging his club around in a circle until Chubbins ducked his head for fear it might hit him.

"You are welcome to our forest," chirped Robin, in a sedate and dignified tone.

"And here is Mr. Goldfinch and his charming bride," continued the policeman.

"Ah, it is a pleasure to meet you," the goldfinch murmured, eyeing the child-larks curiously, but trying to be so polite that they would not notice his staring.

"Henny Wren and Jenny Wren," proceeded the policeman.

Twinkle and Chubbins both bowed politely.

"Well, well!" croaked a raven, in a hoarse voice, "am I to wait all day while you introduce those miserable little insignificant grub-eaters?"

"Be quiet!" cried Policeman Bluejay, sternly.

"I won't," snapped the raven.

It happened so quickly that the children saw nothing before they heard the thump of the club against the raven's head.

"Caw — waw — waw — waw! Murder! Help!" screamed the big bird, and flew away from the tree as swiftly as his ragged wings would carry him.

"Let him go," said a sweet brown mocking-bird. "The rowdy is always disturbing our social gatherings, and no one will miss him if he doesn't come back."

"He is not fit for polite society," added a nuthatcher, pruning her scarlet wings complacently.

So the policeman tucked the club under his wing again and proceeded with the introductions, the pewees and the linnets being next presented to the strangers, and then the comical little chickadees, the orioles, bobolinks, thrushes, starlings and whippoorwills, the latter appearing sleepy because, they explained, they had been out late the night before.

These smaller birds all sat in rows on the limbs beside Twinkle and Chubbins; but seated upon the stouter limbs facing them were rows of bigger birds who made the child-larks nervous by the sharp glances from their round, bright eyes. Here were blackbirds, cuckoos, magpies, grosbeaks and wood-pigeons, all nearly as big and fierce-looking as Policeman Bluejay himself, and some so rugged and strong that it seemed strange they would submit to the orders of the officer of the law. But the policeman kept a sharp watch upon these birds, to see that they attempted no mischievous pranks, and they must have been afraid of him because they behaved very well after the saucy raven had left them. Even the chattering magpies tried to restrain their busy tongues, and the blackbirds indulged in no worse pranks than to suddenly spread their wings and try to push the pigeons off the branch.

Several beautiful humming-birds were poised in the air above this gathering, their bodies being motionless but their tiny wings fluttering so swiftly that neither Twinkle nor Chubbins could see them at all.

Policeman Bluejay, having finally introduced all the company to the child-larks, began to relate the story of their adventures, telling the birds how the wicked tuxix had transformed them into the remarkable shapes they now possessed.

"For the honor of our race," he said, "we must each and every one guard these little strangers carefully, and see that they come to no harm in our forest. You must all pledge yourselves to befriend them on all occasions, and if any one dares to break his promise he must fight with me to the death — and you know very well what that means."

"We do," said a magpie, with a shrill laugh. "You'll treat us as you did Jim Crow. Eh?"

The policeman did not notice this remark, but the other birds all looked grave and thoughtful, and began in turn to promise that they would take care to befriend the child-larks at all times.

This ceremony having been completed, the birds began to converse in a more friendly and easy tone, so that Twinkle and Chubbins soon ceased to be afraid of them, and enjoyed very much their society and friendly chatter.

Chapter 5

The Oriole's Story

"We are really very happy in this forest," said an oriole that sat next to Twinkle, "and we would have no fears at all did not the men with guns, who are called hunters, come here now and then to murder us. They are terribly wild and ferocious creatures, who have no hearts at all."

"Oh, they *must* have hearts," said Twinkle, "else they couldn't live. For one's heart has to beat to keep a person alive, you know."

"Perhaps it's their gizzards that beat," replied the oriole, reflectively, "for they are certainly heartless and very wicked. A cousin of mine, Susie Oriole, had a very brave and handsome husband. They built a pretty nest together and Susie laid four eggs in it that were so perfect that she was very proud of them.

"The eggs were nearly ready to hatch when a great man appeared in the forest and discovered Susie's nest. Her brave husband fought desperately to protect their home, but the cruel man shot him, and he fell to the ground dead. Even then Susie would not leave her pretty eggs, and when the man climbed the tree to get them she screamed and tried to peck out his eyes. Usually we orioles are very timid, you know; so you can well understand how terrified Susie was to fight against this giant foe. But he had a club in his hand, with which he dealt my poor cousin such a dreadful blow that she was sent whirling through the air and sank half unconscious into a bush a few yards away.

"After this the man stole the eggs from the nest, and also picked up the dead body of Susie's husband and carried it away with him. Susie recovered somewhat from the blow she had received, and when she saw her eggs and her poor dead husband being taken away, she managed to flutter along after the man and followed him until he came to the edge of the forest. There he had a horse tied to a tree, and he mounted upon the beast's back and rode away through the open country. Susie followed him, just far enough away to keep the man in sight, without being noticed herself.

"By and by he came to a big house, which he entered, closing the door behind him. Susie flew into a tree beside the house and waited sorrowfully but in patience for a chance to find her precious ones again.

"The days passed drearily away, one after another, but in about a week my cousin noticed that one of the windows of the house had been left open. So she boldly left her tree and flew in at the window, and luckily none of the people who lived in the house happened to be in the room.

"Imagine Susie's surprise when she saw around the sides of the room many birds sitting silently upon limbs cut from trees, and among them her own husband, as proud and beautiful as he had ever been before the cruel man had killed him! She quickly flew to the limb and perched beside her loved one.

" 'Oh, my darling!' she cried, 'how glad I am to have found you again, and to see you alive and well when I had mourned you as dead. Come with me at once, and we will return to our old home in the forest.'

"But the bird remained motionless and made no reply to her loving words. She thrust her bill beside his and tried to kiss him, but he did not respond to the caress and his body was stiff and cold.

"Then Susie uttered a cry of grief, and understood the truth. Her husband was indeed dead, but had been stuffed and mounted upon the limb to appear as he had in life. Small wires had been pushed through his legs to make his poor body stand up straight, and to Susie's horror she discovered that his eyes were only bits of glass! All the other birds in the room were stuffed in the same way. They looked as if they were alive, at the first glance; but each body was cold and every voice mute. They were mere mockeries of the beautiful birds that this heartless and cruel man had deprived of their joyous lives.

"Susie's loving heart was nearly bursting with pain as she slowly fluttered toward the open window by which she had entered. But on her way a new anguish overtook her, for she noticed a big glass case against the wall in which were arranged clusters of eggs stolen from birds of almost every kind. Yes; there were her own lovely eggs, scarcely an inch from her face, but separated from her by a stout glass that could not be broken, although she madly dashed her body against it again and again.

"Finally, realizing her helplessness, poor Susie left the room by the open window and flew back to the forest, where she told us all the terrible thing she had seen. No one was able to comfort her, for her loving heart was broken; and after that she would often fly away to the house to peer through the window at her eggs and her beautiful husband.

"One day she did not return, and after waiting for her nearly two weeks we sent the bluejay to see what had become of her. Our policeman found the house, and also found the window of the room open.

"He boldly entered, and discovered Susie and her husband sitting side by side upon the dried limb, their bodies both stiff and dead. The man had caught the poor wife at last, and the lovers were reunited in death.

"Also Policeman Bluejay found his grandfather's mummy in this room, and the stuffed mummies of many other friends he had known in the forest. So he was very sorrowful when he returned to us, and from that time we have feared the heartless men more than ever."

"It's a sad story," sighed Twinkle, "and I've no doubt it is a true one. But all men are not so bad, I'm sure."

"All men who enter the forest are," answered the oriole, positively. "For they only come here to murder and destroy those who are helpless before their power, but have never harmed them in the least. If God loves the birds, as I am sure He does, why do you suppose He made their ferocious enemies, the men?"

Twinkle did not reply, but she felt a little ashamed.

Chapter 6

A Merry Adventure

"Talking about men," said the cuckoo, in a harsh but not very unpleasant voice, "reminds me of a funny adventure I once had myself. I was sitting in my nest one day, at the time when I was quite young, when suddenly a man appeared before me. You must know that this nest, which was rather carelessly built by my mother, was in a thick evergreen tree, and not very high from the ground; so that I found the man's eyes staring squarely into my own.

"Most of you, my dears, have seen men; but this was the strangest sort of man you can imagine. There was white hair upon his face, so long it hung down to his middle, and over his eyes were round plates of glass that glittered very curiously. I was so astonished at seeing the queer creature that I sat still and stared, and this was my undoing. For suddenly there came a rapid 'whish!' through the air, and a network of cords fell all around and over me. Then, indeed, I spread my wings and attempted to fly; but it was too late. I struggled in the net without avail, and soon gave up the conflict in breathless despair.

"My captor did not intend to kill me, however. Instead, he tried to soothe my fright, and carried me very gently for many, many miles, until we came to a village of houses. Here, at the very top of a high house, the man lived in one little room. It was all littered with tools and bits of wood, and on a broad shelf were several queer things that went 'tick-tock! tick-tock!' every minute. I was thrust, gently enough, into a wooden cage, where I lay upon the bottom more dead than alive because the ticking things at first scared me dreadfully and I was in constant terror lest I should be tortured or killed. But the glass-eyed old man brought me dainty things to eat, and plenty of fresh water to relieve my thirst, and by the next day my heart had stopped going pitty-pat and I was calm enough to stand up in my cage and look around me.

"My white-whiskered captor sat at a bench with his coat off and his bald head bare, while he worked away busily putting little wheels and springs together, and fitting them into a case of wood. When one of them was finished it would sing 'tick-tock! tick-tock!' just like the other queer things on the shelf, and this constant ticking so interested me that I raised my head and called:

" 'Cuck-oo! cuck-oo!'

" 'That's it!' cried the old man, delightedly. 'That's what I wanted to hear. It's the real cuckoo at last, and not a bit like those cheap imitations.'

"I didn't understand at first what he meant, but he worked at his bench all day, and finally brought to my cage a bird made out of wood, that was carved and painted to look just as I was. It seemed so natural that I flapped my wings and called 'cuck-oo' to it, and the man pressed a little bellows at the bottom of the bird and made it say 'cuck-oo!' in return. But that cry was so false and unreal that I just shouted with laughter, and the glass-eyed old man shook his head sadly and said: 'That will never do. That will never do in the world.'

"So all the next day he worked hard trying to make his wooden bird say 'cuck-oo!' in the proper way; and at last it really spoke quite naturally, so that it startled even me when I heard it. This seemed to please my captor very much; so he put it inside one of the ticking things on the shelf, and by-and-by a door opened and the wooden bird jumped out and cried 'Cuck-oo! Cuck-oo! Cuck-oo!' and then jumped back again and the door closed with a snap.

" 'Bravo!' cried old white-hair; but I was rather annoyed, for I thought the wooden bird was impudent in trying to ape the ways of live cuckoos. I shouted back a challenge to it, but there was no reply. An hour later, and every hour, it repeated the performance, but jumped behind the door when I offered to fight it.

"The next day the man was absent from the room, and I had nothing to eat. So I became angry and uneasy. I scratched away at the wooden bars of my cage and tried to twist them with my beak, and at last one of them, to my great joy, came loose, and I was able to squeeze myself out of the cage.

"But then I was no better off than before, because the windows and the door of the room were fast shut. I grew more cross and ill-tempered than before, when I discovered this, and to add to my annoyance that miserable wooden bird would every once in awhile jump out and yell 'Cuck-oo!' and then bounce back into its house again, without daring to argue with me.

"This at last made me frantic with rage, and I resolved to be revenged. The next time the wooden bird made its appearance I flew upon it in a flash and knocked it off the little platform before it had uttered its cry more than twice. It fell upon the floor and broke one of its wings; but in an instant I dashed myself upon it and bit and scratched the impudent thing until there was not a bit of paint left upon it. Its head came off, too, and so did its legs and the other wing, and before I was done with it no one ever would have known it was once a clever imitation of myself. Finding that I was victorious I cried 'Cuck-oo!' in triumph, and just then the little door of the ticking thing opened and the platform where the wooden bird had stood came out of it and remained for a time motionless. I quickly flew up and perched upon it, and shouted 'Cuck-oo!' again, in great glee. As I did so, to my amazement the platform on which I stood leaped backward, carrying me with it, and the next instant the door closed with a snap and I found myself in darkness.

"Wildly I fluttered my wings; but it was of no use. I was in a prison much worse than the cage, and so small that I could hardly turn around in it. I was about to die of terror and despair when I chanced to remember that at certain times the door would open to push out the bird and allow it to say 'Cuck-oo!' before it shut again. So, the next time it opened in this way, I would be able to make my escape.

"Very patiently I waited in the dark little hole, listening to the steady 'tick-tock!' of the machinery behind me and trying not to be nervous. After awhile I heard the old man come into the room and exclaim sorrowfully because his captive cuckoo had escaped from its cage. He could not imagine what had become of me, and I kept still and laughed to myself to think how I would presently surprise him.

"It seemed an age before I finally heard the click that opened the door in front of me. Then the platform on which I sat sprang out, and I fluttered my wings and yelled 'Cuck-oo! Cuck-oo!' as loud as I could. The old man was standing right in front of me, his mouth wide open with astonishment at the wonderfully natural performance of his wooden bird, as he thought me. He shouted 'Bravo!' again, and clapped his hands; and at that I flew straight into his face, and clawed his white hair with all my might, and screamed as loud as I could.

"He screamed, too, being taken by surprise, and tumbled over backward so that he sat down upon the floor with a loud bump. I flew to the work-bench, and then the truth dawned upon him that I was not the wooden bird but the real one.

" 'Good gracious!' said he, 'I've left the window open. The rascal will escape!'

"I glanced at the window and saw that it was indeed wide open. The sight filled me with triumphant joy. Before the old man could get upon his feet and reach the window I had perched upon the sill, and with one parting cry of 'Cuck-oo!' I spread my wings and flew straight into the air.

"Well, I never went back to enquire if he enjoyed the trick I had played upon him, but I've laughed many a time when I thought of the old fellow's comic expression when a real cuckoo instead of a painted one flew out of his ticking machine."

As the cuckoo ended his tale the other birds joined in a chorus of shrill laughter; but Chubbins said to them, gravely:

"He was a smart man, though, to make a cuckoo-clock. I saw one myself, one time, and it was a wonderful thing. The cuckoo told what time it was every hour."

"Was it made of wood?" asked the bluejay.

"I don't know that," replied the boy-lark; "but of course it wasn't a real bird."

"It only shows," remarked the bobolink, "how greatly those humans admire us birds. They make pictures of us, and love to keep us in cages so they can hear us sing, and they even wear us in their bonnets after we are dead."

"I think that is a dreadful thing," said the goldfinch, with a shudder. "But it only proves that men are our greatest enemies."

"Don't forget the women," said Twinkle. "It's the women that wear birds in their hats."

"Mankind," said Robin Redbreast, gravely, "is the most destructive and bloodthirsty of all the brute creation. They not only kill for food, but through vanity and a desire for personal adornment. I have even heard it said that they kill for amusement, being unable to restrain their murderous desires. In this they are more cruel than the serpents."

"There is some excuse for the poor things," observed the bluejay, "for nature created them dependent upon the animals and birds and fishes. Having neither fur nor feathers to protect their poor skinny bodies, they wear clothing made of the fleece of sheep, and skins of seals and beavers and otters and even the humble muskrats. They cover their feet and their hands with skins of beasts; they sleep upon the feathers of birds; their food is the flesh of beasts and birds and fishes. No created thing is so dependent upon others as man; therefore he is the greatest destroyer in the world. But he is not alone in his murderous, despoiling instinct. While you rail at man, my friends, do not forget that birds are themselves the greatest enemies of birds."

"Nonsense!" cried the magpie, indignantly.

"Perhaps the less you say about this matter the better," declared the bluejay, swinging his club in a suggestive manner, and looking sharply at the magpie.

"It's a slander," said the blackbird. "I'm sure you can't accuse *me* of injuring birds in any way."

"If you are all innocent, why are we obliged to have a policeman?" enquired the little wren, in a nervous voice.

"Tell me," said Twinkle, appealing to the bluejay; "are the big birds really naughty to the little ones?"

"Why, it is the same with us as it is with men," replied the policeman. "There are good ones and bad ones among us, and the bad ones have to be watched. Men destroy us wantonly; other animals and the sly serpents prey upon us and our eggs for food; but these are open enemies, and we know how we may best avoid them. Our most dangerous foes are those bandits of our own race who, instead of protecting their brethren, steal our eggs and murder our young. They are not always the biggest birds, by any means, that do these things. The crow family is known to be treacherous, and the shrike is rightly called the 'butcher-bird,' but there are many others that we have reason to suspect feed upon their own race."

"How dreadful!" exclaimed the girl-lark.

The birds all seemed restless and uneasy at this conversation, and looked upon one another with suspicious glances. But the bluejay soothed them by saying:

"After all, I suppose we imagine more evil than really exists, and sometimes accuse our neighbors wrongfully. But the mother birds know how often their nests have been robbed in their absence, and if they suspect some neighbor of the crime instead of a prowling animal it is but natural, since many birds cannot be trusted. There are laws in the forest, of course; but the guilty ones are often able to escape. I'll tell you of a little tragedy that happened only last week, which will prove how apt we are to be mistaken."

Chapter 7

The Bluejay's Story

"There is no more faithful mother in the forest than the blue titmouse, which is a cousin to the chickadee," continued the policeman, "and this spring Tom Titmouse and his wife Nancy set up housekeeping in a little hollow in an elm-tree about half a mile north of this spot. Of course, the first thing Nancy did was to lay six beautiful eggs — white with brown spots all over them — in the nest. Tom was as proud of these eggs as was Nancy, and as the nest was hidden in a safe place they flew away together to hunt for caterpillars, and had no thought of danger. But on their return an hour later what was their sorrow to find the nest empty, and every pretty egg gone. On the ground underneath the tree were scattered a few bits of shell; but the robber was nowhere to be seen.

"Tom Titmouse was very indignant at this dreadful crime, and came to me at once to complain of the matter; but of course I had no idea who had done the deed. I questioned all the birds who have ever been known to slyly steal eggs, and every one denied the robbery. So Nancy Titmouse saw she must lay more eggs, and before long had another six speckled beauties in the bottom of her nest.

"They were more careful now about leaving home; but the danger seemed past. One bright, sunny morning they ventured to fly to the brook to drink and bathe themselves, and on their return found their home despoiled for a second time. Not an egg was left to them out of the six, and while Nancy wept and wailed Tom looked sharply around him and saw a solitary shrike sitting on a limb not far away."

"What's a shrike?" asked Chubbins.

"It is a bird that looks a good deal like that mocking-bird sitting next you; but it bears a bad character in the forest and has earned the vile name of 'butcher-bird.' I admit that I am always obliged to keep an eye upon the shrike, for I expect it to get into mischief at any time. Well, Tom Titmouse naturally thought the shrike had eaten Nancy's eggs, so he came to me and ordered me to arrest the robber. But the shrike pleaded his innocence, and I had no proof against him.

"Again Nancy, with true motherly courage and perseverance, laid her eggs in the nest; and now they were never left alone for a single minute. Either she or Tom was always at home, and for my part I watched the shrike carefully and found he did not fly near the nest of the titmice at all.

"The result of our care was that one fine day the eggs hatched out, and six skinny little titmice, with big heads and small bodies, were nestling against Nancy's breast. The mother thought they were beautiful, you may be sure, and many birds gathered around to congratulate her and Tom, and the brown thrush sang a splendid song of welcome to the little ones.

"When the children got a little stronger it did not seem necessary to guard the nest so closely, and the six appetites required a good many insects and butterfly-eggs to satisfy them. So Tom and Nancy both flew away to search for food, and when they came back they found, to their horror, that their six little ones had been stolen, and the nest was bare and cold. Nancy nearly fainted with sorrow, and her cries were pitiful and heart-rending; but Tom Titmouse was dreadfully angry, and came to me demanding vengeance.

" 'If you are any good at all as a policeman,' said he, 'you will discover and punish the murderer of my babies.'

"So I looked all around and finally discovered, not far from the nest of the titmice, four of their children, all dead and each one impaled upon the thorn of a bush that grew close to the ground. Then I decided it was indeed the shrike, for he has a habit of doing just this thing; killing more than he can eat and sticking the rest of his murdered victims on thorns until he finds time to come back and devour them.

"I was also angry, but that time; so I flew to the shrike's nest and found him all scratched and torn and his feathers plucked in many places.

" 'What has happened to you?' I asked.

" 'I had a fight with a weasel last night,' answered the shrike, 'and both of us are rather used up, today.'

" 'Still,' said I, sternly, 'you had strength enough to kill the six little titmice, and to eat two of them.'

" 'I never did,' said he, earnestly; 'my wings are too stiff to fly.'

" 'Do not lie about it, I beg of you,' said I; 'for we have found four of the dead titmice stuck on the thorns of a bush, and your people have been known to do such things before.'

"At this the shrike looked worried.

" 'Really,' said he, 'I cannot understand it. But I assure you I am innocent.'

"Nevertheless, I arrested him, and made him fly with me to the Judgment Tree, where all the birds had congregated. He was really stiff and sore, and I could see it hurt him to fly; but my duty was plain. We selected a jury of twelve birds, and Judge Bullfinch took his seat on a bough, and then the trial began.

"Tom Titmouse accused the shrike of murder, and so did Nancy, who had nearly cried her eyes out. I also gave my evidence. But the prisoner insisted strongly that he was innocent, and claimed he had not left his nest since his fight with the weasel, and so was guiltless of the crime.

"But no one had any sympathy for him, or believed what he said; for it is often the case that when one has earned a bad character he is thought capable of any wickedness. So the jury declared him guilty, and the judge condemned him to die at sundown. We were all to fall upon the prisoner together, and tear him into bits with bill and claw; but while we waited for the sun to sink Will Sparrow flew up to the Judgment Tree and said:

" 'Hello! What's going on here?'

" 'We are just about to execute a criminal,' replied the judge.

" 'What has he been doing?' asked Will, eyeing the shrike curiously.

" 'He killed the titmice children this morning, and ate two of them, and stuck the other four upon a thorn bush,' explained the judge.

" 'Oh, no; the shrike did not do that!' cried Will Sparrow. 'I saw the crime committed with my own eyes, and it was the cunning weasel — the one that lives in the pine stump — that did the dreadful murder.'

"At this all the birds set up an excited chatter, and the shrike again screamed that he was innocent. So the judge said, gravely: 'Will Sparrow always speaks the truth. Release the prisoner, for we have misjudged him. We must exact our vengeance upon the weasel.'

"So we all flew swiftly to the pine stump, which we knew well, and when we arrived we found the weasel sitting at the edge of his hole and laughing at us.

" 'That is the very weasel I fought with,' said the shrike. 'You can see where I tore the fur from his head and back with my sharp beak.'

The trial of the shrike

" 'So you did,' answered the weasel; 'and in return I killed the little tomtits.'

" 'Did you stick them on the thorns?' asked Judge Bullfinch.

" 'Yes,' said the weasel. 'I hoped you would accuse the shrike of the murder, and kill him to satisfy my vengeance.'

" ' We nearly fell into the trap,' returned the judge; 'but Will Sparrow saw your act and reported it just in time to save the shrike's life. But tell me, did you also eat Nancy Titmouse's eggs?'

" 'Of course,' confessed the weasel, 'and they were very good, indeed.'

"Hearing this, Tom Titmouse became so excited that he made a furious dash at the weasel, who slipped within his hole and escaped.

" 'I condemn you to death!' cried the judge.

" 'That's all right,' answered the weasel, sticking just the tip of his nose out of the hole. 'But you've got to catch me before you can kill me. Run home, my pretty birds. You're no match for a weasel!'

"Then he was gone from sight, and we knew he was hidden safely in the stump, where we could not follow him, for the weasel's body is slim and slender. But I have not lived in the forest all my life without learning something, and I whispered a plan to Judge Bullfinch that met with his approval. He sent messengers at once for the ivory-billed woodpeckers, and soon four of those big birds appeared and agreed to help us. They began tearing away at the stump with their strong beaks, and the splinters flew in every direction. It was not yet dark when the cunning weasel was dragged from his hole and was at the mercy of the birds he had so cruelly offended. We fell upon him in a flash, and he was dead almost instantly."

"What became of the shrike?" asked Twinkle.

"He left the forest the next day," answered Policeman Blue-jay. "For although he was innocent of this crime, he was still a butcher-bird, and he knew our people had no confidence in him."

"It was lucky Will Sparrow came in time," said the girl-lark. "But all these stories must have made you hungry, so I'd like to invite my guests to have some refreshments."

The birds seemed much surprised by this invitation, and even Policeman Bluejay wondered what she was going to do. But Twinkle whispered to Chubbins, and both the bird-children flew into their basket and returned with their claws full of cookie. They repeated the journey many times, distributing bits of the rare food to all of the birds who had visited them, and each one ate the morsel eagerly and declared that it was very good.

"Now," said the policeman, when the feast was over, "let us all go to the brook and have a drink of its clear, sweet water."

So they flew away, a large and merry band of all sizes and colors; and the child-larks joined them, skimming the air as lightly and joyously as any of their new friends. It did not take them long to reach a sparkling brook that wound its way through the forest, and all the feathered people drank their fill standing upon the low bank or upon stones that rose above the level of the water.

At first the children were afraid they might fall into the brook; but presently they gained courage, and when they saw the thrush and bullfinch plunge in and bathe themselves in the cool water Chubbins decided to follow their example, and afterward Twinkle also joined them.

The birds now bade the child-larks good-bye and promised to call upon them again, and soon all had flown away except the bluejay, who said he would see Twinkle and Chubbins safe home again, so that they would not get lost.

They thanked him for this kindness, and when they had once more settled upon the limb beside their nest the bluejay also bade them good night and darted away for one last look through the forest to see that all was orderly for the night.

Chapter 8

Mrs. Hootaway

As the child-larks sat side by side upon their limb, with the soft gray nest near at hand, the twilight fell and a shadow began to grow and deepen throughout the forest.

"Twink," said Chubbins, gravely, "how do you like it?"

"Well," replied the girl, "it isn't so bad in the daytime, but it's worse at night. That bunch of grass mixed up with the stems of leaves, that they call a nest, isn't much like my pretty white bed at home, Chubbins."

"Nor mine," he agreed. "And, Twink, how ever can we say our prayers when we haven't any hands to hold up together?"

"Prayers, Chub," said the girl, "are more in our hearts than in our hands. It isn't what we *do* that counts; it's what we feel. But the most that bothers me is what the folks at home will think, when we don't come back."

"They'll hunt for us," Chubbins suggested; "and they may come under this tree, and call to us."

"If they do," said Twinkle, "we'll fly right down to them."

"I advise you not to fly much, in the night," said a cheery voice beside them, and Wisk the squirrel stuck his head out of the hollow where he lived. "You've had quite a party here today," he continued, "and they behaved pretty well while the policeman was around. But some of them might not be so friendly if you met them alone."

"Would any bird hurt us?" asked the girl, in surprise.

"Why, I've seen a magpie meet a thrush, and fly away alone," replied Wisk. "And the wrens and chickadees avoid the cuckoo as much as possible, because they are fond of being alive. But the policeman keeps the big birds all in order when he is around, and he makes them all afraid to disobey the laws. He's a wonderful fellow, that Policeman Bluejay, and even we squirrels are glad he is in the forest."

"Why?" asked Chubbins.

"Well, we also fear some of the birds," answered Wisk. "The lady in the third flat, for instance, Mrs. Hootaway, is said to like a squirrel for a midnight meal now and then, when mice and beetles are scarce. It is almost her hour for wakening, so I must be careful to keep near home."

"Tut — tut — tut!" cried a harsh voice from above. "What scandal is this you are talking, Mr. Wisk?"

The squirrel was gone in a flash; but a moment later he put out his head again and turned one bright eye toward the upper part of the tree. There, on a perch outside her hollow, sat the gray owl, pruning her feathers. It was nearly dark by this time, and through the dusk Mrs. Hootaway's yellow eyes could be seen gleaming bright and wide open.

"What nonsense are you putting into the heads of these little innocents?" continued the owl, in a scolding tone.

"No nonsense at all," said Wisk, in reply. "The child-larks are safe enough from you, because they are under the protection of Policeman Bluejay, and he would have a fine revenge if you dared to hurt them. But my case is different. The laws of the birds do not protect squirrels, and when you're abroad, my dear Mrs. Hootaway, I prefer to remain snugly at home."

"To be sure," remarked the owl, with a laugh. "You are timid and suspicious by nature, my dear Wisk, and you forget that although I have known you for a long time I have never yet eaten you."

"That is my fault, and not yours," retorted the squirrel.

"Well, I'm not after you tonight, neighbor, nor after birds, either. I know where there are seven fat mice to be had, and until they are all gone you may cease to worry."

"I'm glad to hear that," replied Wisk. "I wish there were seven hundred mice to feed your appetite. But I'm not going to run into danger recklessly, nevertheless, and it is my bed-time. So good night, Mrs. Hootaway; and good night, little child-larks."

The owl did not reply, but Twinkle and Chubbins called good night to the friendly squirrel, and then they hopped into their nest and cuddled down close together.

The moon was now rising over the trees and flooding the gloom of the forest with its subdued silver radiance. The children were not sleepy; their new life was too strange and wonderful for them to be able to close their eyes at once. So they were rather pleased when the gray owl settled on the branch beside their nest and began to talk to them.

"I'm used to slanders, my dears," she said, in a pleasanter tone than she had used before, "so I don't mind much what neighbor Wisk says to me. But I do not wish you to think ill of the owl family, and so I must assure you that we are as gentle and kindly as any feathered creatures in the forest — not excepting the Birds of Paradise."

"I am sure of that," replied Twinkle, earnestly. "You are too soft and fluffy and pretty to be bad."

"It isn't the prettiness," said the gray owl, evidently pleased by the compliment. "It is the nature of owls to be kind and sympathetic. Those who do not know us very well say harsh things about us, because we fly in the night, when most other birds are asleep, and sleep in the daytime when most other birds are awake."

"Why do you do that?" asked Chubbins.

"Because the strong light hurts our eyes. But, although we are abroad in the night, we seek only our natural prey, and obey the Great Law of the forest more than some others do."

"What is the Great Law?" enquired Twinkle, curiously.

"Love. It is the moral law that is above all laws made by living creatures. The whole forest is ruled by love more than it is by fear. You may think this is strange when you remember that some animals eat birds, and some birds eat animals, and the dreadful creeping things eat us both; but nevertheless we are so close to Nature here that love and tenderness for our kind influences us even more than it does mankind — the careless and unthinking race from which you came. The residents of the forest are good parents, helpful neighbors, and faithful friends. What better than this could be said of us?"

"Nothing, I'm sure, if it is true," replied the girl.

"Over in the Land of Paradise," continued the owl, thoughtfully, "the birds are not obliged to take life in order to live themselves; so they call us savage and fierce. But I believe our natures are as kindly as those of the Birds of Paradise."

"Where is this Land of Paradise you speak of?" asked Twinkle.

"Directly in the center of our forest. It is a magical spot, protected from intrusion not by any wall or barred gates, but by a strong wind that blows all birds away from that magnificent country except the Birds of Paradise themselves. There is a legend that man once lived there, but for some unknown crime was driven away. But the birds have always been allowed to inhabit the place because they did no harm."

"I'd like to see it," said Chubbins.

"So would I," confessed the gray owl, with a sigh; "but there is no use of my attempting to get into the Paradise of Birds, because the wind would blow me back. But now it is getting quite dark, and I must be off to seek my food. Mrs. 'Possum and I have agreed to hunt together, tonight."

"Who is Mrs. 'Possum?" the girl asked.

"An animal living in the lowest hollow of this tree, answered the owl. "She is a good-natured creature, and hunts by night, as I do. She is slow, but, being near the ground, she can spy a mouse much quicker than I can, and then she calls to me to catch it. So between us we get plenty of game and are helpful to each other. The only drawback is that Mrs. 'Possum has four children, which she carries in her pouch wherever she goes, and they have to be fed as well as their mother. So the 'possums have five mouths to my one, and it keeps us busy to supply them all."

"It's very kind of you to help her," remarked Twinkle.

"Oh, she helps me, too," returned the owl, cheerfully. "But now good night, my dears. You will probably be sound asleep when I get home again."

Off flew Mrs. Hootaway with these words, and her wings moved so noiselessly that she seemed to face away into the darkness like a ghost.

The child-larks sat looking at the silver moon for a time; but presently Twinkle's eyelids drooped and she fell fast asleep, and Chubbins was not long in following her example.

Chapter 9

The Destroyers

A loud shouting and a bang that echoed like a clap of thunder through the forest awoke the bird-children from their dreams.

Opening their eyes with a start they saw that the gray dawn was breaking and a sort of morning twilight made all objects in the forest distinct, yet not so brilliant as the approaching daylight would. Shadows still lay among the bushes and the thickest branches; but between the trees the spaces were clearly visible.

The children, rudely awakened by the riot of noise in their ears, could distinguish the barking of dogs, the shouts of men calling to the brutes, and the scream of an animal in deep distress. Immediately after, there was a whirl overhead and the gray owl settled on the limb beside their nest.

"They've got her!" she exclaimed, in a trembling, terrified voice. "The men have shot Mrs. 'Possum dead, and the dogs are now tearing her four babies limb from limb!"

"Where are they?" whispered Twinkle, her little heart beating as violently as if the dread destroyers had always been her mortal enemies.

"Just below us. Isn't it dreadful? We had such a nice night together, and Mrs. 'Possum was so sweet and loving in caring for her little ones and feeding them! And, just as we were nearly home again, the dogs sprang upon my friend and the men shot her dead. We had not even suspected, until then, that our foes were in the forest."

Twinkle and Chubbins craned their necks over the edge of the nest and looked down. On the ground stood a man and a boy, and two great dogs were growling fiercely and tearing some bloody, revolting object with their cruel jaws.

"Look out!" cried the voice of Wisk, the squirrel. "He's aiming at you — look out!"

They ducked their heads again, just as the gun roared and flamed fire beneath them.

"Oh-h-h!" wailed Mrs. Hootaway, fluttering violently beside them. "They struck me that time — the bullet is in my heart. Good-bye, my dears. Remember that — all — is love; all is — love!"

Her voice died away to a whisper, and she toppled from the limb. Twinkle and Chubbins tried to save their dying friend from falling, but the gray owl was so much bigger than they that they could not support the weight of her body. Slowly she sank to the ground and fell upon the earth with a dull sound that was dreadful to hear.

Instantly Twinkle darted from the nest and swooped downward, alighting on the ground beside the owl's quivering body. A big dog came bounding toward her. The man was reloading his gun, a few paces away.

"Call off your dog!" shouted Twinkle, wildly excited. "How dare you shoot the poor, harmless birds? Call off your dog, I say!"

But, even as she spoke, the words sounded in her own ears strange and unnatural, and more like the chirping of a bird than the language of men. The hunter either did not hear her or he did not understand her, and the dog snarled and bared its wicked teeth as it sprang greedily upon the child-lark.

Twinkle was too terrified to move. She glared upon the approaching monster helplessly, and it had almost reached her when a black object fell from the skies with the swiftness of a lightning streak and struck the dog's back, tearing the flesh with its powerful talons and driving a stout, merciless beak straight through the skull of the savage brute.

The dog, already dead, straightened out and twitched convulsively. The man shouted angrily and sprang upon the huge bird that had slain his pet, at the same time swinging his gun like a club.

"Quick!" said the eagle to Twinkle, "mount with me as swiftly as you can."

With the words he rose into the air and Twinkle darted after him, while Chubbins, seeing their flight from his nest, joined them just in time to escape a shot from the boy's deadly gun.

The inquisitive squirrel, however, had stuck his head out to see what was happening, and one of the leaden bullets buried itself in his breast. Chubbins saw him fall back into his hollow and heard his agonized scream; but he could not stay to help his poor friend. An instant later he had joined the eagle and Twinkle, and was flying as hard and swift as his wonderful lark wings could carry him up, up into the blue sky.

The sunshine touched them now, while below the tragic forest still lay buried in gloom.

"We are quite safe here, for I am sure no shot from a gun could reach us," said the eagle. "So let us rest upon our wings for a while. How lucky it was that I happened to be around in time to rescue you, my little friends."

"I am very grateful, indeed," answered Twinkle, holding her wings outstretched so that she floated lightly in the air beside her rescuer. "If you had been an instant later, the dog would have killed me."

"Very true," returned the eagle. "I saw your danger while I was in the air, and determined to act quickly, although I might myself have been shot by the man had his gun been loaded. But I have noticed that a bold action is often successful because it causes surprise, and the foe does not know what to do."

"I'm 'shamed of those people," said Chubbins, indignantly. "What right had they to come to the forest and kill the pretty owl, and the dear little squirrel, and the poor mama 'possum and her babies?"

"They had the right of power," said the eagle, calmly. "It would be a beautiful world where there no destroyers of life in it; but the earth and air and water would then soon become so crowded that there would not be room for them all to exist. Don't blame the men."

"But they are cruel," said Twinkle, "and kill innocent, harmless birds and animals, instead of the wicked ones that could be better spared."

"Cruelty is man's nature," answered the eagle. "Of all created things, men, tigers and snakes are known to be the most cruel. From them we expect no mercy. But now, what shall be our next movement? I suppose it will be best for you to keep away from the forest until the men are gone. Would you like to visit my home, and meet my wife and children?"

"Yes, indeed!" cried Twinkle; "if you will be kind enough to let us."

"It will be a great pleasure to me," said the eagle. "Follow me closely, please."

He began flying again, and they kept at his side. By and by they noticed a bright, rosy glow coming from a portion of the forest beneath them.

"What is that?" asked Chubbins.

"It is the place called the Paradise of Birds," answered their conductor. "It is said to be the most beautiful place in all the world, but no one except the Birds of Paradise are allowed to live there. Those favored birds sometimes enter our part of the forest, but we are never allowed to enter theirs."

"I'd like to see that place," said Twinkle.

"Well, you two child-larks are different from all other birds," remarked the eagle, "and for that reason perhaps you would be allowed to visit the paradise that is forbidden the rest of us. If ever I meet one of the beautiful birds that live there, I will ask it to grant you the privilege."

"Do!" said Twinkle and Chubbins, in one eager breath.

They flew for a long time, high in the air, but neither of the bird-children seemed to tire in the least. They could not go quite as fast as the eagle, however, who moderated his speed so that they could keep up with him.

Chapter 10

In the Eagle's Nest

Gradually the forest passed out of sight and only bleak, rugged mountains were below them. One peak rose higher than the others, and faced the sea, and to this point the great eagle directed their flight.

On a crag that jutted out from the mountain was the eagle's nest, made of rude sticks of wood gathered from the forest. Sitting beside the nest was Mrs. Eagle, larger and more pompous even than her husband, while squatting upon the edge of the nest were two half-grown eaglets with enormous claws and heads, but rather skinny bodies that were covered with loose and ragged feathers. Neither the nest nor the eaglets appeared to be very clean, and a disagreeable smell hung over the place.

"This is funny," said Mrs. Eagle, looking at the child-larks with surprise. "Usually you kill your game before you bring it home, Jonathan; but today it seems our dinner has flown to us willingly."

"They're for us!" cried one of the eaglets, making a quick dash to seize Twinkle, who darted out of his reach.

"One for each of us!" screamed the other eaglet, rushing at Chubbins.

"Peace — be quiet!" said the eagle, sternly. "Cannot you tell friends from food, you foolish youngsters? These are two little friends of mine whom I have invited to visit us; so you must treat them in a civil manner."

"Why not eat them?" asked one of the eaglets, looking at the child-larks with hungry eyes.

"Because I forbid you. They are my guests, and must be protected and well treated. And even if this were not so, the larks are too small to satisfy your hunger, you little gluttons."

"Jonathan," said Mrs. Eagle, coldly, "do not reproach our offspring for their hunger. We sent you out this morning to procure a supply of food, and we expected you to bring us home something good to eat, instead of these useless little creatures."

The eagle seemed annoyed at being scolded in this manner.

"I had an adventure in the forest," he said, "and came near being shot and killed by a man. That is the reason I came home so soon."

Twinkle and Chubbins were standing together at the edge of the crag when one of the eaglets suddenly spread out his wide, stiff wings and pushed them over the precipice. They recovered themselves before they had fallen far, and flew to the ledge again just in time to see the father eagle cuff his naughty son very soundly. But the mother only laughed in her harsh voice and said:

"It is so early in the day, Jonathan, that I advise you to go again in search of food. Our sweet darlings will not be comforted until they have eaten."

"Very well," answered the eagle. "I am sorry you cannot treat my guests more politely, for they are all unaccustomed to such rudeness. But I see that it will be better for me to take them away with me at once."

"Do," said Mrs. Eagle; and the eaglets cried: "Better let us eat 'em, daddy. They are not very big, but they're better than no breakfast at all."

"You're dis'greeable things!" said Twinkle, indignantly; "and I don't like you a bit. So *there!*"

"Come on, Twink," said Chubbins. "Let's go away."

"I will take you back to the forest," the eagle declared, and at once rose into the air. Twinkle and Chubbins followed him, and soon the nest on the crag was left far behind and they could no longer hear the hoot of the savage young ones.

For a time the eagle flew in silence. Then he said:

"You must forgive my family for not being more hospitable. You must know that they live a very lonely life, and have no society because every living thing fears them. But I go abroad more and see more of the world, so I know very well how guests ought to be treated."

"You have been very kind to us, Mr. Eagle," replied the girl-lark, "and you saved my life when the dog would have killed me. I don't blame *you* any for what your family did. My mama says lots of people show off better abroad than they do at home, and that's your case exactly. If I were you I wouldn't take any more visitors to my nest."

"I do not intend to," answered the eagle. "But I am glad that you think well of me personally, if you do not of my family, and I assure you it has been a real pleasure to me to assist you. Were you like ordinary birds, you would be beneath my notice; but I am wise enough to understand that you are very unusual and wonderful little creatures, and if at any time I can serve you further, you have but to call me, and I will do what I can for you."

"Thank you very much," replied Twinkle, who realized that the great bird had acted more gently toward them than it is the nature of his wild race to do.

They had just reached the edge of the forest again when they saw a bird approaching them at a great speed, and soon it came near enough for them to see that it was Policeman Bluejay. He wore his official helmet and carried his club, and as soon as he came beside them he said:

"Thank goodness I've found you at last. I've been hunting for you an hour, and began to fear you had met with some misfortune."

"We've been with the eagle," said the girl. "He saved our lives and carried us away from where the dreadful men were."

"We have had sad doings in the forest today — very sad, in-deed," declared the bluejay, in a grave voice. "The hunters did even more damage than usual. They killed Jolly Joe, the brown bear, and Sam Fox, and Mrs. 'Possum and her babies, and Wisk the squirrel; so that the animals are all in mourning for their friends. But our birds suffered greatly, also. Mrs. Hootaway is dead, and three pigeons belonging to a highly respected family; but the saddest of all is the murder of Mr. and Mrs. Goldfinch, both of whom were killed by the same shot. You may remember, my dears, that they were at your reception yesterday, and as gay and happy as any of the company present. In their nest are now five little children, too young and weak to fly, and there is no one to feed them or look after them."

"Oh, that is dreadful!" exclaimed Twinkle. "Can't Chubbins and I do something for the little goldfinches?"

"Why, that is why I was so anxious to find you," answered Policeman Bluejay. "You haven't laid any eggs yet, and have no one to depend upon you. So I hoped you would adopt the goldfinch babies."

"We will," said Chubbins, promptly. "We can feed them out of our basket."

"Oh, yes," chimed in the girl. "We couldn't catch grubs for them, you know."

"It won't be necessary," observed the policeman, with a sly wink at the eagle. "They're too young yet to know grubs from grub."

Chapter 11

The Orphans

The eagle now bade them good-bye and flew away in search of prey, while the bluejay and the child-larks directed their flight toward that part of the great forest where they lived.

"Are you sure the men have gone?" asked Chubbins.

"Yes," replied the policeman; "they left the forest as soon as they had shot Jolly Joe, for the brown bear was so heavy that they had to carry him on a pole resting across their shoulders. I hope they won't come again very soon."

"Did they take Mrs. Hootaway with them?" asked Twinkle.

"Yes; she will probably be stuffed, poor thing!"

Presently they passed near the rosy glow that lighted up the center of the forest with its soft radiance, and the girl said:

"That is the Paradise Land, where the Birds of Paradise live. The eagle has promised to ask one of those birds to let us visit their country."

"Oh, I can do better than that, if you wish to visit the Paradise," responded the bluejay; "for the Guardian of the Entrance is a special friend of mine, and will do whatever I ask him to."

"Will he, really?" asked the girl, in delight.

"To be sure. Some day I will take you over there, and then you will see what powerful friends Policeman Bluejay has."

"I'd like that," declared Twinkle.

Their swift flight enabled them to cover the remaining distance very rapidly, and soon they were at home again.

They first flew to the nest of the goldfinches, which was in a tree not far from the maple where the lark-children lived. There they found the tiny birds, who were yet so new that they were helpless indeed. Mrs. Redbreast was sitting by the nest when they arrived, and she said:

"The poor orphans are still hungry, although I have fed them all the insects I could find near. But I am glad that you have come, for it is time I was at home looking after my own little ones."

"Chubbins and I have 'dopted the goldfinches," said Twinkle, "so we will look after them now. But it was very nice of you, Mrs. Redbreast, to take care of them until we arrived."

"Well, I like to be neighborly," returned the pretty bird; "and as long as cruel men enter our forest no mother can tell how soon her own little ones will be orphaned and left helpless."

"That is true," said the policeman, nodding gravely.

So Mrs. Redbreast flew away and now Chubbins looked curiously into the nest, where several fluffy heads were eagerly lifted with their bills as wide open as they could possibly stretch.

"They must be just *awful* hungry, Twink," said the boy.

"Oh, they're always like that," observed Policeman Bluejay, calmly. "When anyone is around they open their mouths to be fed, whether they are hungry or not. It's the way with birdlets."

"What shall we feed them?" asked Twinkle.

"Oh, anything at all; they are not particular," said the bluejay, and then he flew away and left the child-larks to their new and interesting task.

"I'll be the father, and you be the mother," said Chubbins.

"All right," answered Twinkle.

"Peep! peep! peep!" said the tiny goldfinches.

"I wonder if the luncheon in our basket would agree with them," remarked the girl, looking at the open mouths reflectively as she perched her own brown body upon the edge of the deep nest.

"Might try it," suggested the boy. "The cop says they're not particular, and what's good enough for us ought to be good enough for them."

So they flew to where the basket hung among the thick leaves of the tree, which had served to prevent the men from discovering it, and crept underneath the cloth that covered it.

"Which do you think they'd like best," asked Chubbins, "the pickles or the cheese?"

"Neither one," Twinkle replied. "The sandwiches will be best for them. Wait; I'll pick out some of the meat that is between the slices of bread. They'll be sure to like that."

"Of course," agreed Chubbins, promptly. "They'll think it's bugs."

So each one dragged out a big piece of meat from a sandwich, and by holding it fast in one claw they managed to fly with the burden to the nest of the goldfinch babies.

"Don't give it to 'em all at once," cautioned the girl. "It would choke 'em."

"I know," said Chubbins.

He tore off a tiny bit of the meat and dropped it into one of the wide-open bills. Instantly it was gone and the mouth was open again for more. They tried to divide the dinner equally among them, but they all looked so alike and were so ravenous to eat everything that was dropped into their bills that it was hard work to keep track of which had been fed and which had not. But the child-larks were positive that each one had had enough to keep it from starving, because there was a big bunch in front of each little breast that was a certain proof of a full crop.

The next task of the guardians was to give the birdlets drink; so Twinkle and Chubbins flew to the brook and by hunting around a while they found an acorn-cup that had fallen from one of the oak trees. This they filled with water, and then Twinkle, who was a trifle larger than the boy-lark, clutched the cup firmly with her toes and flew back to the orphans without spilling more than a few drops. They managed to pour some of the water into each open mouth, and then Twinkle said:

"There! they won't die of either hunger or thirst in a hurry, Chub. So now we can feed ourselves."

"Their mouths are still open," returned the boy, doubtfully.

"It must be a habit they have, she answered. "Wouldn't you think they'd get tired stretching their bills that way?"

"Peep! peep! peep!" cried the baby goldfinches.

"You see," said the boy, with a wise look, "they don't know any better. I had a dog once that howled every time we shut him up. But if we let him alone he stopped howling. We'll go and get something to eat and let these beggars alone a while. Perhaps they'll shut their mouths by the time we get back again."

"May be," replied Twinkle.

They got their own luncheon from the basket, and afterward perched on the tree near the nest of the little goldfinches. They did not feel at all comfortable in their old nest in the maple, because they could not forget the tragic deaths of the inhabitants of the three hollows in the tree — the three "flats" as poor Wisk had merrily called them.

During the afternoon several of the birds came to call upon the orphans, and they all nodded approval when they found the child-larks watching over the little ones. Twinkle questioned some of the mothers anxiously about that trick the babies had of keeping their bills open and crying for food, but she was told to pay no attention to such actions.

Nevertheless, the pleadings of the orphans, who were really

stuffed full of food, made the child-larks so nervous that they hailed with delight the arrival of Policeman Bluejay in the early evening. The busy officer had brought with him Mrs. Chaffinch, a widow whose husband had been killed a few days before by a savage wildcat.

Mrs. Chaffinch declared she would be delighted to become a mother to the little goldfinches, and rear them properly. She had always had good success in bringing up her own children, she claimed, and the goldfinches were first cousins to the chaffinches, so she was sure to understand their ways perfectly.

Twinkle did not want to give up her charges at first, as she had become interested in them; but Chubbins heaved a sigh of relief and declared he was glad the "restless little beggars" had a mother that knew more about them than he did. The bluejay hinted that he considered the widow's experience would enable her to do more for the baby goldfinches than could a child-lark who had never yet laid an egg, and so Twinkle was forced to yield to his superior judgment.

Mrs. Chaffinch settled herself in a motherly manner upon the nest, and the two bird-children bade her good-night and returned to their own maple tree, where they had a rather wakeful night, because Chubbins thoughtlessly suggested that the place might be haunted by the ghosts of the gray owl, Wisk, and Mrs. 'Possum.

But either the poor things had no ghosts or they were too polite to bother the little child-larks.

Chapter 12

The Guardian

The next morning ushered in a glorious day, sunny and bright. The sky was a clear blue, and only a slight breeze ruffled the leaves of the trees. Even before Twinkle and Chubbins were awake the birds were calling merrily to one another throughout the forest, and the chipmonks chirped in their own brisk, businesslike way as they scuttled from tree to tree.

While the child-larks were finishing their breakfast Policeman Bluejay came to them, his feathers looking fresh and glossy and all his gorgeous colorings appearing especially beautiful in the sunshine.

"Today will be a rare day to visit the Paradise," he said; "so I have come to escort you to the Guardian of the Entrance, who I am sure will arrange for you to enter that wonderful country."

"It is very kind of you to remember our wish," said Twinkle. "We are all ready."

So they flew above the tree-tops and began their journey toward the center of the forest.

"Where's your p'liceman's hat and club?" Chubbins asked the bluejay.

"Why, I left them at home," was the reply. "I'm not on official duty today, you know, and the Guardian does not like to see anything that looks like a weapon. In his country there are no such things as quarrels or fighting, or naughtiness of any sort; for as they have everything they want there is nothing to quarrel over or fight for. The Birds of Paradise have laws, I understand; but they obey them because they are told to, and not because they are forced to. It would be a bad country for a policeman to live in."

"But a good place for everyone else," said Twinkle.

"Perhaps so," agreed the policeman, reluctantly. "But I sometimes think the goody-goody places would get awful tiresome to live in, after a time. Here in our part of the forest there is a little excitement, for the biggest birds only obey our laws through fear of punishment, and I understand it is just the same in the world of men. But in the Birds' Paradise there lives but one race, every member of which is quite particular not to annoy any of his fellows in any way. That is why they will admit no disturbing element into their country. If you are admitted, my dears, you must be very careful not to offend any one that you meet."

"We'll try to be good," promised Chubbins.

"I would not dare to take any of my own people there," continued the bluejay, flying swiftly along as they talked together; "but you two are different, and more like the fairy Birds of Paradise themselves than like our forest birds. That is the reason I feel sure the Guardian will admit you."

"I'm naughty sometimes, and so is Chubbins," said Twinkle, honestly. "But we try not to be any naughtier than we can help."

"I am sure you will behave very nicely," replied the bluejay.

After a time the rosy glow appeared reflected in the blue sky, and as they flew toward it the soft and delightful radiance seemed to grow and deepen in intensity. It did not dazzle their eyes in the least, but as the light penetrated the forest and its furthest rays fell upon the group, they experienced a queer sense of elation and light-hearted joy.

But now the breeze freshened and grew more strong, pressing against their feathered breasts so gently yet powerfully that they soon discovered they were not advancing at all, but simply fluttering in the air.

"Drop down to the ground," whispered the bluejay; and they obeyed his injunction and found that close to the earth the wind was not so strong.

"That is a secret I learned some time ago," said their friend. "Most birds who seek to enter the Paradise try to beat against the wind, and are therefore always driven back; but there is just one way to approach the Guardian near enough to converse with him. After that it depends entirely upon his good-will whether you get any farther."

The wind still blew so strong that it nearly took their breath away, but by creeping steadily over the ground they were able to proceed slowly, and after a time the pressure of the wind grew less and less, until it suddenly ceased altogether.

Then they stopped to rest and to catch their breaths, but before this happened Twinkle and Chubbins both uttered exclamations of amazement at the sight that met their eyes.

Before them was a grove composed of stately trees not made of wood, but having trunks of polished gold and silver and leaves of exquisite metallic colorings. Beneath the trees was a mass of brilliant flowers, exceedingly rare and curious in form, and as our little friends looked upon them these flowers suddenly began a chant of greeting and then sang a song so sweet and musical that the lark-children were entranced and listened in rapt delight.

When the song ended the flowers all nodded their heads in a pretty way, and Twinkle drew a long breath and murmured:

"Isn't it odd to hear flowers sing? I'm sure the birds themselves cannot beat that music."

"They won't try," replied the policeman, "for Birds of Paradise do not sing."

"How strange!" exclaimed the girl.

"The land they live in is so full of music that they do not need to," continued the bluejay. "But before us is the entrance, leading through the limbs of that great golden tree you see at the left. Fly swiftly with me, and perch upon the middle branch."

With these words he darted toward the tree, and Twinkle and Chubbins followed. In a few seconds they alighted upon the branch and found themselves face to face with the first Bird of Paradise they had yet seen.

He possessed a graceful carriage and a most attractive form, being in size about as large as a common pigeon. His eyes were shrewd but gentle in expression and his pose as he stood regarding the newcomers was dignified and impressive. But the children had little time to note these things because their wondering eyes were riveted upon the bird's magnificent plumage. The feathers lay so smoothly against his body that they seemed to present a solid surface, and in color they were a glistening emerald green upon the neck and wings, shading down on the breast to a softer green and then to a pure white. The main wing-feathers were white, tipped with vivid scarlet, and the white feathers of his crest were also tipped with specks of flame. But his tail feathers were the most beautiful of all his gay uniform. They spread out in the shape of a fan, and every other feather was brilliant green and its alternate feather snow white.

"How lovely!" cried Twinkle, and the bird bowed its head and with a merry glance from its eyes responded:

"Your admiration highly honors me, little stranger."

"This," said Policeman Bluejay, "is the important official

called the Guardian of the Entrance of Paradise. Sir Guardian, permit me to introduce to you two children of men who have been magically transformed into skylarks against their will. They are not quite birds, because their heads retain the human shape; but whatever form they may bear, their natures are sweet and innocent and I deem them worthy to associate for a brief time with your splendid and regal race. Therefore I have brought them here to commend them to your hospitality and good-will, and I hope you will receive them as your guests."

"What are your names, little strangers?" asked the Guardian.

"Mama calls me Twinkle," said the girl.

"I'm Chubbins," said the boy.

The Guardian looked attentively at the bluejay.

"You know our regulations," said he; "no birds of the forest are admitted to our Paradise."

"I know," replied the policeman. "I will await my little friends here. It is pleasure enough for me to have just this glimpse of your beautiful fairyland."

The Guardian nodded his approval of this speech.

"Very well," he answered, "you shall remain and visit with me. If all forest birds were like you, my friend, there would be little danger in admitting them into our society. But they are not, and the laws must be regarded. As for the child-larks, I will send them first to the King, in charge of the Royal Messenger, whom I will now summon."

He tossed his head upward with an abrupt motion, and in the tree-top a chime of golden bells rang musically in the air. The flowers beneath them caught up the refrain, and sang it softly until another bird came darting through the air and alighted on the golden limb beside the Guardian.

The newcomer was differently garbed from the other. His plumage was orange and white, the crest and wing-feathers being tipped with bright blue. Nor was he so large as the Guardian, nor so dignified in demeanor. Indeed, his expression was rather merry and roguish, and as he saw the strangers he gave a short, sharp whistle of surprise.

"My dear Ephel," said the Guardian, "oblige me by escorting these child-larks to the presence of his Majesty the King."

"I am delighted to obey your request," answered Ephel the Messenger, brightly. Then, turning to Twinkle and Chubbins, he added: "I trust you will find my society agreeable during our flight to the royal monarch of Paradise."

Twinkle was too much embarrassed by this politeness to answer at once, but Chubbins said "Sure thing!" in a matter-of-fact voice, and the Messenger nodded gaily and continued:

"Then we will go, if it pleases you."

He spread his wings in a flash of color and sped away into the Paradise, and the children eagerly followed him.

Chapter 13

The King Bird

More and more magnificence was unfolded as they advanced into this veritable fairyland of the birds. Vines of silver climbed up the golden trunks of trees and mingled their twining threads with the brilliant leaves. And now upon the trees appeared jewelled blossoms that sparkled most exquisitely in the rosy-hued radiance that, in this favored spot, had taken the place of sunshine. There were beds of plants with wide-spreading leaves that changed color constantly, one hue slowly melting into another and no two leaves on the same plant having the same color at the same time. Yet in spite of the vivid coloring that prevailed everywhere, each combination seemed in perfect harmony and served to delight the sense.

Bushes that emitted a grateful fragrance bore upon slender branches little bells that at times tinkled in the perfumed breeze and played sweet melodies, while here and there were clusters of fountain-lilies that shot sprays of crystal water high into the air. When the water fell back again and the drops struck against the broad leaves of the plants, they produced a melodious sound that was so delightful that Twinkle thought she could listen to it for hours.

Their guide flew silently on, and the two children were so much amazed by their surroundings that they had no words for questions or even remarks.

The scene was ever shifting and becoming more and more lovely and fascinating, and the paradise was more extensive than they had thought it.

By and by Ephel the Messenger approached the central part, where was a great arbor thickly covered with masses of pure white flowers. Some of these were large, like chrysanthemums and mammoth white double roses, while among them were twined smaller and more delicate blossoms, like the bells of lilies-of-the-valley.

Ephel entered the arch of the arbor and flew on, for it was of great extent and continually enlarged from the point of entrance, so that at last the child-larks found themselves in a lofty circular chamber banked on sides and roof with solid masses of the snow-white flowers, which filled the air with a sweet and agreeable perfume. The floor was also a mass of white blossoms, so that the place resembled the inside of a huge cornucopia.

But the eyes of the little strangers were not directed so much to the arbor itself as to the group of splendid birds that occupied the flower-chamber and perched upon a wide-spreading bush of filigree gold that rose from the middle of the floor and spread its dainty branches in every direction.

On the lower branches sat many birds of marvelous colorings, some having blue the predominant tint in their feathers, and others green, or scarlet, or brilliant yellows. In strong contrast with these were a few modest-looking birds with soft brown feathers covering their graceful forms, that sat silently upon the lowest and most retired branch of the golden bush; but still greater was the contrast of all present with the magnificence of the one occupying the topmost branch.

This gorgeous creature, whose splendor dominated the white bower, at once won the children's attention, and they had no doubt they were gazing upon the King Bird of Paradise.

The feathers of his head and neck were so fine that they

looked like a covering of velvet. These seemed to be, at first, of a delicate lavender color, but the children observed that they shone with a different tint at every movement the King made. The body feathers, also as glossy as velvet, were of a rich royal purple, shading to lavender, and then to white upon his breast. His wing plumes were white, tipped with specks of lustrous gold.

But by far the most astonishing part of the King's plumage was that which consisted of the dainty, fern-like plumes that rose from his body and tail and spread in graceful and bewildering curves both right and left, until his form seemed to be standing in a feathery bower of resplendent beauty. All the colors of the rainbow were seen in these delicate feathers, and against the white background of the arch this monarch of the feathered world appeared more royally magnificent than any words can describe.

Both Twinkle and Chubbins gasped with amazement and delight as, at the command of Ephel, they alighted upon a lowly branch of the golden bush and bowed their heads before the ruler of the birds' fairyland.

"Ah, whom have we here?" asked the King, in a soft voice, as he strutted and proudly turned himself upon his perch.

"Strangers, your Majesty," answered the Messenger. "They are sent to you by the Guardian of the Entrance because they are gentle and innocent, and are neither birds nor mortals, but a part of both."

"They are certainly very curious," remarked the King, staring at the human heads upon the lark bodies. "May I ask you, little strangers, how you happen to exist in your present form?"

Twinkle, tossing her head to throw back a straggling lock of hair that had fallen across her eyes, began in her sweet voice to tell the story of their enchantment, and not only the King but all the Birds of Paradise present listened intently to her words.

When she had finished the King exclaimed:

"Indeed, my dear child-larks, you are worthy to be our guests in fairyland. So it will please me if you will be as happy and comfortable as possible, and enjoy your stay with us as much as you can. My people will delight to honor and amuse you, and Ephel shall continue to guide you wherever you go."

"Thank you," returned Twinkle, earnestly; and Chubbins added, in his blunt way: "Much obliged."

"But, before you go," continued his Majesty, "tell me what you think of my royal person. Am I not beautiful?"

"You are, indeed," replied Twinkle; "only — "

"Only what?" asked the King, as she hesitated.

"Only I'm sorry you are so vain, and strut around so, and want everyone to see how beautiful you are."

"Why should I not? Is not vanity one of the great virtues?" asked the King, in a surprised voice.

"My mama says people ought not to think themselves nice, or pretty," said the child. "With us, to be vain is a fault, and we are taught to be modest and unassuming."

"How remarkable!" exclaimed the King. "And how very thoughtless your mother must be. Here we think that if God creates us beautiful it is a sin not to glory in His work, and make everyone acknowledge the kindly skill of the Supreme Maker's hand. Should I try to make others think, or should I myself think, that I am not most gracefully formed and most gorgeously clothed, I would be guilty of the sin of not appreciating the favor of God, and deserve to be punished."

Twinkle was amazed, but could find no words to contradict this astonishing idea.

"I had not thought of it in that way," she answered. "Perhaps I am wrong, your Majesty; and certainly you are very beautiful."

"Think it over," said the King, graciously. "Learn to be grateful for every good thing that is yours, and proud that you have been selected by Nature for adornment. Only in this way may such rare favors be deserved. And now the royal Messenger will show you the sights of our Paradise, and try to entertain you pleasantly while you are our guests."

He turned aside, with these words, and fluttered his waving feathers so that their changing tints might dazzle the eyes of all observers. But immediately afterward he paused and cried out:

"Dear me! One of my wing plumes is disarranged. Help me, you ladies!"

At once the small brown birds on the lower branches, who had been modestly quiet because they had no gay plumage, flew up to the King and with their bills skillfully dressed his feathers, putting the wing plume into its place again and arranging it properly, while the other birds looked on with evident interest.

As the lark-children turned away to follow the Messenger Chubbins remarked:

"I'm glad *I* haven't got all those giddy feathers."

"Why?" asked Twinkle, who had been rather awed by the King's splendor.

"Because it would take all my time to keep 'em smooth," answered the boy. "The poor King can't do much more than admire himself, so he don't get time to have fun."

Chapter 14

A Real Fairyland

As they left the royal arbor of white flowers the Messenger turned to the left and guided his guests through several bright and charming avenues to a grove of trees that had bright blue bark and yellow leaves. Scattered about among the branches were blossoms of a delicate pink color, shaped like a cup and resembling somewhat the flower of the morning-glory.

"Are you hungry?" asked Ephel.

"Oh, I could eat something, I guess," said Chubbins.

The Messenger flew to one of the trees and alighted upon a branch where three of the pink, cup-shaped flowers grew in a row. The children followed him, and sitting one before each blossom they looked within the cups and found them filled with an unknown substance that both looked and smelled delicious and appetizing.

"It is royal amal," said their guide, busily pecking at his cup with his bill. "Help yourselves, little ones. You will find it very nice indeed."

"Well," said Twinkle, "I'd be glad to eat it if I could. But it wouldn't do Chubbins and me a bit of good to stick our noses into these cups."

Ephel turned to look at them.

"True," he remarked; "it was very careless of me to forget that you have no bills. How are you accustomed to eat?"

"Why, with spoons, and knives and forks," said the girl.

"You have but to ask for what you need," declared the royal Messenger.

Twinkle hesitated, scarcely knowing what to say. At last she spoke boldly: "I wish Chub and I had spoons."

Hardly had the words left her lips when two tiny golden spoons appeared in the flower-cups. Twinkle seized the spoon before her in one claw and dipped up a portion of the strange food, which resembled charlotte russe in appearance. When she tasted it she found it delicious; so she eagerly ate all that the blossom contained.

When she looked around for Chubbins she found he was gone. He had emptied his cup and carried the golden spoon to another blossom on a higher limb, where the girl discovered him eating as fast as he could dip up the food.

"Let us go to another tree," said Ephel. "There are many excellent things to eat, and a variety of food is much more agreeable than feasting upon one kind."

"All right," called Chubbins, who had succeeded in emptying the second cup.

As they flew on Twinkle said to the guide:

"I should think the blossoms would all be emptied in a little while."

"Oh, they fill up again in a few moments," replied Ephel. "Should we go back even now, I think we would find them all ready to eat again. But here are the conona bushes. Let us taste these favorite morsels."

The bushes on which they now rested had willow-green branches with silver balls growing thickly upon them. Ephel tapped lightly upon one of the balls with his bill and at once it opened by means of a hinge in the center, the two halves of the ball lying flat, like plates. On one side Twinkle found tiny round pellets of cake, each one just big enough to make a mouthful for a bird. On the other side was a thick substance that looked like jelly.

"The proper thing to do," said their guide, "is to roll one of the pellets in the jelly, and then eat it."

He showed Twinkle how to do this, and as she had brought her golden spoon with her it was easy enough. Ephel opened a ball for Chubbins and then one for himself, and the children thought this food even nicer than the first they had eaten.

"Now we will have some fruit," declared the Messenger. He escorted his charges to an orchard where grew many strange and beautiful trees hanging full of fruits that were all unknown to the lark-children. They were of many odd shapes and all superbly colored, some gleaming like silver and gold and others being cherry-red or vivid blue or royal purple in shade. A few resembled grapes and peaches and cherries; but they had flavors not only varied and delicious but altogether different from the fruits that grow outside of the Birds' Paradise.

Another queer thing was, that as fast as the children ate one fruit, another appeared in its place, and they hopped from branch to branch and tree to tree, trying this one and that, until Chubbins exclaimed:

"Really, Twink, I can't eat another mouthful."

"I'm afraid we've both been stuffing ourselves, Chub," the girl replied. "But these things taste so good it is hard to stop at the right time."

"Would you like to drink?" asked Ephel.

"If you please," Twinkle answered.

"Then follow me," said the guide.

He led them through lovely vistas of wonderful trees, down beautiful winding avenues that excited their admiration, and past clusters of flowering plants with leaves as big as umbrellas

235

and as bright as a painter's palette. The Paradise seemed to have been laid out according to one exquisite, symmetrical plan, and although the avenues or paths between the trees and plants led in every direction, the ground beneath them was everywhere thickly covered with a carpet of magnificent flowers or richly tinted ferns and grasses. This was because the birds never walked upon the ground, but always flew through the air.

Often, as they passed by, the flowers would greet them with sweet songs or choruses and the plants would play delightful music by rubbing or striking their leaves against one another, so that the children's ears were constantly filled with harmony, while their eyes were feasted on the bewildering masses of rich color, and each breath they drew was fragrant with the delicious odors of the blossoms that abounded on every side.

"Of all the fairylands I've ever heard of or read about," said Twinkle, "this certainly is the best."

"It's just a peach of a fairyland," commented Chubbins, approvingly.

"Here is the nectar tree," presently remarked the royal Messenger, and he paused to allow them to observe it.

The tree was all of silver — silver trunk and branches and leaves — and from the end of each leaf or branch dripped sparkling drops of a pink-tinted liquid. These glistened brightly as they fell through the air and lost themselves in a bed of silver moss that covered all the ground beneath the tree.

Ephel flew to a branch and held his mouth open so that a drop from above fell into it. Twinkle and Chubbins followed his example, and found the pink liquid very delightful to drink. It seemed to quench their thirst and refresh them at the same time, and when they flew from the queer dripping tree they were as light-hearted and gay as any two children so highly favored could possibly have felt.

"Haven't you any water in your paradise?" asked the little girl-lark.

"Yes, of course," Ephel answered. "The fountain-lilies supply what water we wish to drink, and the Lustrous Lake is large enough for us all to bathe in. Besides these, we have also the Lake of Dry Water, for you must know that the Lustrous Lake is composed of wet water."

"I thought all water was wet," said Chubbins.

"It may be so in your country," replied the Royal Messenger, "but in our Paradise we have both dry and wet water. Would you like to visit these lakes?"

"If you please," said Twinkle.

Chapter 15

The Lake of Dry Water

They flew through the jeweled gardens for quite a way, emerging at last from among the trees to find before them a pretty sheet of water of a greenish hue. Upon the shore were rushes that when swayed by the breeze sang soft strains of music.

"This," announced their guide, "is the Lake of Dry Water."

"It *looks* wet, all right," said Chubbins, in a tone of doubt.

"But it isn't," declared Ephel. "Watch me, if you please."

He hovered over the lake a moment and then dove downward and disappeared beneath the surface. When he came up again he shook the drops of water from his plumage and then flew back to rejoin his guests.

"Look at me," he said. "My feathers are not even damp."

They looked, and saw that he spoke truly. Then Chubbins decided to try a bath in the dry water, and also plunged into the lake. When he came to the surface he floated there for a time, and ducked his head again and again; but when he came back to the others not a hair of his head nor a feather of his little brown body was in the least moist.

"That's fine water," said the boy-lark. "I suppose you Birds of Paradise bathe here all the time."

"No," answered Ephel; "for only wet water is cleansing and refreshing. We always take our daily baths in the Lustrous Lake.

But here we usually sail and disport ourselves, for it is a comfort not to get wet when you want to play in the water."

"How do you sail?" asked Twinkle, with interest.

"I will show you," replied their guide.

He flew to a tall tree near, that had broad, curling leaves, and plucked a leaf with his bill. The breeze caught it at once and wafted it to the lake, so that it fell gently upon the water.

"Get aboard, please," called Ephel, and alighted upon the broad surface of the floating leaf. Twinkle and Chubbins followed, one sitting in front of their guide and one behind him. Then Ephel spread out his wings of white and orange, and the breeze pushed gently against them and sent the queer boat gliding over the surface of the dry water.

"Sometimes, when the wind is strong," said the Royal Messenger, "these frail craft upset, and then we are dumped into the water. But we never mind that, because the water is dry and we are not obliged to dress our feathers again."

"It is very convenient," observed Twinkle, who was enjoying the sail. "Could one be drowned in this lake?"

"I suppose an animal, like man, could, for it is as impossible to breathe beneath dry water as it is beneath wet. But only birds live here, and they cannot drown, because as soon as they come to the surface they fly into the air."

"I see," said Twinkle, musingly.

They sailed way across the lake, and because the wind was gentle they did not upset once. On reaching the farther shore they abandoned the leaf-boat and again took wing and resumed their flight through the avenues.

There was a great variety of scenery in the Paradise, and wherever they went something new and different was sure to meet their view.

At one place the avenue was carpeted with big pansies of every color one could imagine, some of them, indeed, having several colors blended together upon their petals. As they passed over the pansies Twinkle heard a chorus of joyous laughter, and looking downward, she perceived that the pansies all had faces, and the faces resembled those of happy children.

"Wait a minute," she cried to Chubbins and the guide, and then she flew downward until she could see the faces more plainly. They smiled and nodded to the girl-lark, and laughed their merry laughter; but when she spoke to them Twinkle found they were unable to answer a single word.

Many of the faces were exceedingly beautiful; but others were bold and saucy, and a few looked at her with eyes twinkling with mischief. They seemed very gay and contented in their paradise, so Twinkle merely kissed one lovely face that smiled upon her and then flew away to rejoin her companions.

Chapter 16

The Beauty Dance

Before long they came to another and larger sheet of water, and this Twinkle decided was the most beautiful lake she had ever seen. Its waters were mostly deep blue in color, although they had a changeable effect and constantly shifted from one hue to another. Little waves rippled all over its surface, and the edges of the waves were glistening jewels which, as they scattered in spray and fell into the bosom of the lake, glinted and sparkled with a thousand flashing lights. Here were no rushes upon the shore, but instead of them banks of gorgeous flowers grew far down to the water's edge, so that the last ones dipped their petals into the lake itself.

Nestling upon this bank of flowers the Royal Messenger turned to his companions and said:

"Here let us rest for a time, while I call the friendly fishes to entertain you."

He ended his speech with a peculiar warble, and at its sound a score of fishes thrust their head above the surface of the water. Some of them were gold-fish and some silver-fish, but others had opal tints that were very pretty. Their faces were jolly in expression and their eyes, Chubbins thought, must be diamonds, because they sparkled so brightly.

Swimming softly here and there in the lovely waters of the Lustrous Lake, the fishes sang this song:

"We are the fishes of the lake;
Our lives are very deep;
We're always active when awake
And quiet when asleep.

"We get our fins from Finland,
From books we get our tales;
Our eyes they come from Eyerland
And weighty are our scales.

"We love to flop and twist and turn
Whenever 'tis our whim.
Yet social etiquette we learn
Because we're in the swim.

"Our beds, though damp, are always made;
We need no fires to warm us;
When we swim out we're not afraid,
For autos cannot harms us.

"We're independent little fish
And never use umbrellas.
We do exactly as we wish
And live like jolly fellows."

As the fishes concluded their song they leaped high into the air and then plunged under the water and disappeared, and it was hard to tell which sparkled most brilliantly, their gold and silver bodies or the spray of jewels they scattered about them as they leaped.

"If you should dive into this lake," said Ephel the Messenger, "your feathers would be dripping wet when you came out again. It is here we Birds of Paradise bathe each morning, after which we visit the Gleaming Glade to perform our Beauty Dance."

"I should like to see that glade," said Twinkle, who was determined to let nothing escape her that she could possibly see.

"You shall," answered Ephel, promptly. "We will fly there at once."

So he led the way and presently they entered a thicker grove of trees than any they had before noticed. The trunks were so close together that the birds could only pass between them in single file, but as they proceeded in this fashion it was not long before they came to a circular space which the child-lark knew at once must be the Gleaming Glade.

The floor was of polished gold, and so bright that as they stood upon it they saw their forms reflected as in a mirror. The trees surrounding them were also of gold, being beautifully engraved with many attractive designs and set with rows of brilliant diamonds. The leaves of the trees, however, were of burnished silver, and bore so high a gloss that each one served as a looking-glass, reproducing the images of those standing in the glade thousands of times, whichever way they chanced to turn.

The gleam of these mirror-like leaves was exceedingly brilliant, but Ephel said this radiance was much stronger in the morning, when the rosy glow of the atmosphere was not so powerful.

"Then," said he, "the King Bird and all the Nobility of Paradise, who rejoice in the most brilliant plumage, come here from their bath and dance upon the golden floor the Beauty Dance, which keeps their blood warm until the feathers have all dried. While they dance they can admire their reflections in the mirrors, which adds greatly to their pleasure."

"Don't they have music to dance by?" asked Chubbins.

"Of course," the Messenger replied. "There is a regular orchestra that plays exquisite music for the dance; but the musicians are the female Birds of Paradise, who, because their plumage is a modest brown, are not allowed to take part in the Beauty Dance."

"I think the brown birds with the soft gray breasts are just as pretty as the gaily clothed ones," said Twinkle. "The male birds are too bright, and tire my eyes."

Ephel did not like this speech, for he was very proud of his own gorgeous coloring; but he was too polite to argue with his guest, so he let the remark pass.

"You have now witnessed the most attractive scenes in our favored land," he said; "but there are some curious sights in the suburbs that might serve to interest you."

"Oh! have you suburbs, too?" she asked.

"Yes, indeed. We do not like to come into too close contact with the coarse, outer world, so we have placed the flying things that are not birds midway between our Paradise and the great forest. They serve us when we need them, and are under our laws and regulations; but they are so highly favored by being permitted to occupy the outer edge of our glorious Paradise that they willingly obey their masters. After all, they live happy lives, and their habits, as I have said, may amuse you."

"Who are they?" enquired Chubbins.

"Come with me, and you shall see for yourselves."

They flew away from the grove of the Gleaming Glade and Ephel led them by pleasant routes into a large garden with many pretty flowers in it. Mostly it was filled with hollyhocks — yellow, white, scarlet and purple.

Chapter 17

The Queen Bee

As they approached they heard a low, humming sound, which grew louder as they advanced and aroused their curiosity.

"What is it?" asked Twinkle, at last.

Ephel answered: "It is the suburb devoted to the bees."

"But bees are not birds!" exclaimed Twinkle.

"No; as I have told you, the suburbs contain flying things that cannot be called birds, and so are unable to live in our part of the Paradise. But because they have wings, and love all the flowers and fruits as we do ourselves, we have taken them under our protection."

Ephel perched upon a low bush, and when the child-larks had settled beside him he uttered a peculiar, shrill whistle. The humming sound grew louder, then, and presently hundreds of great bees rose above the flower tops and hovered in the air. But none of them approached the bush except one monstrous bumble-bee that had a body striped with black and gold, and this one sailed slowly toward the visitors and alighted gracefully upon a branch in front of them.

The bee was all bristling with fine hairs and was nearly half as big as Twinkle herself; so the girl shrank back in alarm, and cried:

"Oh-h-h! I'm afraid it will sting me!"

"How ridiculous!" answered the bee, laughing in a small but merry voice. "Our stings are only for our enemies, and we have no enemies in this Paradise; so we do not use our stingers at all. In fact, I'd almost forgotten I had one, until you spoke."

The words were a little mumbled, as if the insect had something in its mouth, but otherwise they were quite easy to understand.

"Permit me to introduce her Majesty the Queen Bee," said their guide. "These, your highness, are some little child-larks who are guests of our King. I have brought them to visit you."

"They are very welcome," returned the Queen Bee. "Are you fond of honey?" she asked, turning to the children.

"Sometimes," replied Chubbins; "but we've just eaten, and we're chock full now."

"You see," the Queen remarked, "my people are all as busy as bees gathering the honey from every flower."

"What do you do with it?" asked Twinkle.

"Oh, we eat part of it, and store up the rest for a rainy day."

"Does it ever rain here?" enquired Chubbins.

"Sometimes, at night, when we are all asleep, so as to refresh and moisten the flowers, and help them to grow."

"But if it rains at night, there can't be any rainy days," remarked Twinkle; "so I can't see the use of saving your honey."

"Nor can I," responded the Queen, laughing again in her pleasant way. "Out in the world people usually rob us of our stores, and so keep us busy getting more. But here there are not even robbers, so that the honey has been accumulating until we hardly know what to do with it. We have built a village of honey-combs, and I have just had my people make me a splendid palace of honey. But it is our way to gather the sweet stuff, whether we need it or not, so we have to act according to our natures. I think of building a mountain of honey next."

"I'd like to see that honey palace," said Twinkle.

"Then come with me," answered the Queen Bee, "for it will give me pleasure to show it to you."

"Shall we go?" asked the girl-lark, turning to Ephel.

"Of course," he returned. "It is quite a wonderful sight, and may interest you."

So they all flew away, the Queen Bee taking the lead, and passed directly over the bed of flowers with its swarm of buzzing, busy bees.

"They remind me of a verse from 'Father Goose,' " said Twinkle, looking curiously but half fearfully at the hundreds of big insects.

"What is the verse?" asked the Queen.

"Why, it goes this way," answered the girl:

" 'A bumble-bee was buzzing on a yellow hollyhock
When came along a turtle, who at the bee did mock,
Saying "Prithee, Mr. Bumble, why make that horrid noise?
It's really distracting, and every one annoys."

" ' "I'm sorry," said, quite humble, the busy droning bee,
"The noise is just my bumble, and natural, you see.
And if I didn't buzz so I'm sure that you'll agree
I'd only be a big fly, and not a bumble-bee." ' "

"That is quite true," said the bee, "and describes our case exactly. But you should know that we are not named 'bumble-bees' by rights, but 'Humble Bees.' The latter is our proper name."

"But why 'humble?' " asked Twinkle.

"Because we are common, work-a-day people, I suppose, and not very aristocratic," was the reply. "I've never heard why they changed our name to 'bumble,' but since you recited that verse I imagine it is on account of the noise our wings make."

They had now passed over the flower beds and approached a remarkable village, where the houses were all formed of golden-yellow honey-combs. There were many pretty shapes among these houses, and some were large and many stories in height while others were small and had but one story. Some had spires and minarets reaching up into the air, and all were laid out into streets just like a real village.

But in the center stood a great honey-comb building with so many gables and roofs and peaks and towers that it was easy to guess it was the Queen Bee's palace, of which she had spoken.

They flew in at a second-story window and found themselves in a big room with a floor as smooth as glass. Yet it was composed of many six-sided cells filled with honey, which could be seen through the transparent covering. The walls and roof were of the same material, and at the end of the room was a throne shaped likewise of the honey cells, like everything else. On a bench along the wall sat several fat and sleepy-looking bumble-bees, who scarcely woke up when their queen entered.

"Those are the drones," she said to her visitors. "It is useless to chide them for their laziness, because they are too stupid to pay attention to even a good scolding. Don't mind them in any way."

After examining the beautiful throne-room, they visited the sleeping chambers, of which there were many, and afterward the parlors and dining-room and the work-rooms.

In these last were many bees building the six-sided pockets or cells for storing the honey in, or piling them up in readiness for the return of those who were gathering honey from the flowers.

"We are not really honey-bees," remarked the Queen; "but gathering honey is our chief business, after all, and we manage to find a lot of it."

"Won't your houses melt when it rains?" asked Twinkle.

"No, for the comb of the honey is pure wax," the Queen Bee replied. "Water does not melt it at all."

"Where do you get all the wax?" Chubbins enquired.

"From the flowers, of course. It grows on the stamens, and is a fine dust called pollen, until we manufacture it into wax. Each of my bees carries two sacks, one in front of him, to put the honey in, and one behind to put the wax in."

"That's funny," said the boy-lark.

"I suppose it may be, to you," answered the Queen, "but to us it is a very natural thing."

Chapter 18

Good News

E phel and the children now bade the good-natured Queen Bee good-bye, and thanked her for her kindness. The Messenger led them far away to another place that he called a "suburb," and as they emerged from a thick cluster of trees into a second flower garden they found the air filled with a great assemblage of butterflies, they being both large and small in size and colored in almost every conceivable manner.

Twinkle and Chubbins had seen many beautiful butterflies, but never such magnificent ones as these, nor so many together at one time. Some of them had wings fully as large as those of the Royal Messenger himself, even when he spread them to their limit, and the markings of these big butterfly wings were more exquisite than those found upon the tail-feathers of the proudest peacocks.

The butterflies paid no attention to their visitors, but continued to flutter aimlessly from flower to flower. Chubbins asked one of them a question, but got no reply.

"Can't they talk?" he enquired of Ephel.

"Yes," said the Messenger, "they all know how to talk, but when they speak they say nothing that is important. They are brainless, silly creatures, for the most part, and are only interesting because they are beautiful to look at. The King likes to watch the flashes of color as they fly about, and so he permits them to live in this place. They are very happy here, in their way, for there is no one to chase them or to stick pins through them when they are caught."

Just then a chime of bells tinkled far away in the distance, and the Royal Messenger listened intently and then said:

"It is my summons to his Majesty the King. We must return at once to the palace."

So they flew into the air again and proceeded to cross the lovely gardens and pass through the avenues of jeweled trees and the fragrant orchards and groves until they came at last to the royal bower of white flowers.

The child-larks entered with their guide and found the gorgeous King Bird of Paradise still strutting on his perch on the golden bush and enjoying the admiring glances of his courtiers and the ladies of his family. He turned as the children entered and addressed his Messenger, saying:

"Well, my dear Ephel, have you shown the strangers all the sights of our lovely land?"

"Most of them, your Majesty," replied Ephel.

"What do you think of us now?" asked the King, turning his eyes upon the lark-children.

"It must be the prettiest place in all the world!" cried Twinkle, with real enthusiasm.

His Majesty seemed much pleased.

"I am very sorry you cannot live here always," he said.

"I'm not," declared Chubbins. "It's too pretty. I'd get tired of it soon."

"He means," said Twinkle, hastily, for she feared the blunt remark would displease the kindly King, "that he isn't really a bird, but a boy who has been forced to wear a bird's body. And your Majesty is wise enough to understand that the sort of life you lead in your fairy paradise would be very different from the life that boys generally lead."

"Of course," replied the King. "A boy's life must be a dreadful one."

"It suits me, all right," said Chubbins.

The King looked at him attentively.

"Would you really prefer to resume your old shape, and cease to be a bird?" he asked.

"Yes, if I could," Chubbins replied.

"Then I will tell you how to do it," said the King. "Since you told me your strange story I have talked with my Royal Necromancer, who knows a good deal about magic, and especially about that same tuxix who wickedly transformed you in the forest. And the Royal Necromancer tells me that if you can find a tingle-berry, and eat it, you will resume your natural form again. For it is the one antidote in all the world for the charm the tuxix worked upon you."

"What *is* a tingle-berry?" asked Twinkle, anxiously, for this information interested her as much as it did Chubbins.

"I do not know," said the King, "for it is a common forest berry, and never grows in our paradise. But doubtless you will have little trouble finding the bush of the tingle-berry when you return to the outside world."

The children were both eager to go at once and seek the tingle-berry; but they could not be so impolite as to run away just then, for the King announced that he had prepared an entertainment in their honor.

So they sat on a branch of the golden bush beside their friend Ephel, while at a nod from the King a flock of the beautiful Birds of Paradise flew into the bower and proceeded to execute a most delightful and bewildering set of aerial evolutions. They flew swiftly in circles, spirals, triangles, and solid squares, and all the time that they performed sweet music was played by some unseen band. It almost dazzled the eyes of the child-larks to watch this brilliant flashing of the colored wings of the birds, but the evolutions only lasted for a few minutes, and then the birds flew out again in regular ranks.

Then the little brown lady-birds danced gracefully upon the carpet, their dainty feet merely touching the tips of the lovely flowers. Afterward the flowers themselves took part, and sang a delightful chorus, and when this was finished the King said they would now indulge in some refreshment.

Instantly a row of bell-shaped blossoms appeared upon the golden bush, one for each bird present, and all were filled with a delicious ice that was as cold and refreshing as if it had just been taken from a freezer. Twinkle and Chubbins asked for spoons, and received them quickly; but the others all ate the ices with their bills.

The King seemed to enjoy his as much as any one, and Twinkle noticed that as fast as a blossom was emptied of its contents it disappeared from the branch.

The child-larks now thanked the beautiful but vain King very earnestly for all his kindness to them, and especially for telling them about the tingle-berries; and when all the good-byes had been exchanged Ephel flew with them back to the tree where they had left the Guardian of the Entrance and their faithful comrade, Policeman Bluejay.

Chapter 19

The Rebels

They were warmly greeted by the bluejay, who asked:
"Did you enjoy the wonderful Paradise?"

"Very much, indeed," cried Twinkle. "But we were sorry you could not be with us."

"Never mind that," returned the policeman, cheerfully. "I have feasted my eyes upon all the beauties visible from this tree, and my good friend the Guardian has talked to me and given me much good advice that will surely be useful to me in the future. So I have been quite contented while you were gone."

The children now gave their thanks to Ephel for his care of them and polite attention, and the Royal Messenger said he was pleased that the King had permitted him to serve them. They also thanked the green-robed Guardian of the Entrance, and then, accompanied by Policeman Bluejay, they quitted the golden tree and began their journey back to the forest.

It was no trouble at all to return. The wind caught their wings and blew against them strongly, so that they had but to sail before the breeze and speed along until they were deep in the forest again. Then the wind moderated, and presently died away altogether, so that they were forced to begin flying in order to continue their journey home.

It was now the middle of the afternoon, and the policeman said:

"I hope all has been quiet and orderly during my absence. There are so many disturbing elements among the forest birds that I always worry when they are left alone for many hours at a time."

"I'm sure they have behaved themselves," returned Twinkle. "They fear your power so much that the evil-minded birds do not dare to offend you by being naughty."

"That is true," said the policeman. "They know very well that I will not stand any nonsense, and will always insist that the laws be obeyed."

They were now approaching that part of the forest where they lived, and as the policeman concluded his speech they were surprised to hear a great flutter of wings among the trees, and presently a flock of big black rooks flew toward them.

At the head of the band was a saucy-looking fellow who wore upon his head a policeman's helmet, and carried under his wing a club.

Policeman Bluejay gave a cry of anger as he saw this, and dashed forward to meet the rooks.

"What does this mean, you rascal?" he demanded, in a fierce voice.

"Easy there, my fine dandy," replied the rook, with a hoarse laugh. "Don't get saucy, or I'll give you a rap on the head!"

The rooks behind him shrieked with delight at this impudent speech, and that made the mock policeman strut more absurdly than ever.

The bluejay was not only astonished at this rebellion but he was terribly angry as well.

"That is my policeman's helmet and club," he said sternly. "Where did you get them?"

"At your nest, of course," retorted the other. "We made up our minds that we have had a miserable bluejay for a policeman long enough; so the rooks elected me in your place, and I'm going to make you birds stand around and obey orders, I can tell you! If you do as I command, you'll get along all right; if you don't, I'll pound you with your own club until you obey."

Again the rooks screamed in an admiring chorus of delight, and when the bluejay observed their great numbers, and that they were all as large as he was, and some even larger and stronger, he decided not to risk an open fight with them just then, but to take time to think over what had best be done.

"I will call the other birds to a meeting," he said to the rook, "and let them decide between us."

"That won't do any good," was the reply. "We rooks have decided the matter already. We mean to rule the forest, after this, and if any one, or all of the birds, dare to oppose us, we'll fight until we force them to serve us. Now, then, what do you intend to do about it?"

"I'll think it over," said Policeman Bluejay.

"Oho! oho! He's afraid! He's a coward!" yelled the rooks; and one of them added:

"Stand up and fight, if you dare!"

"I'll fight your false policeman, or any one of you at a time," replied the bluejay.

"No, you won't; you'll fight us all together, or not at all," they answered.

The bluejay knew it would be foolish to do that, so he turned away and whispered to the lark-children:

"Follow me, and fly as swiftly as you can."

Like a flash he darted high into the air, with Twinkle and Chubbins right behind him, and before the rooks could recover from their surprise the three were far away.

Then the big black birds gave chase, uttering screams of rage;

but they could not fly so swiftly as the bluejay and the larks, and were soon obliged to abandon the pursuit.

When at last he knew that they had escaped the rooks, Policeman Bluejay entered the forest again and went among the birds to call them all to a meeting. They obeyed the summons without delay, and were very indignant when they heard of the rebellion of the rooks and the insults that had been heaped upon their regularly elected officer. Judge Bullfinch arrived with his head bandaged with soft feathers, for he had met the rook policeman and, when he remonstrated, had been severely pounded by the wicked bird's club.

"But what can we do?" he asked. "The rooks are a very powerful tribe, and the magpies and cuckoos and blackbirds are liable to side with them, if they seem to be stronger than we are."

"We might get all our people together and fall upon them in a great army, and so defeat them," suggested an oriole.

"The trouble with that plan," decided the judge, "is that we can only depend upon the smaller birds. The big birds might desert us, and in that case we would be badly beaten."

"Perhaps it will be better to submit to the rooks," said a little chickadee, anxiously. "We are neither warriors nor prize-fighters, and if we obey our new rulers they may leave us in peace."

"No, indeed!" cried a linnet. "If we submit to them they will think we are afraid, and will treat us cruelly. I know the nature of these rooks, and believe they can only be kept from wickedness by a power stronger than their own."

"Hear me, good friends," said the bluejay, who had been silent because he was seriously thinking; "I have a plan for subduing these rebels, and it is one that I am sure will succeed. But I must make a long journey to accomplish my purpose. Go now quietly to your nests; but meet me at the Judgment

Tree at daybreak to-morrow morning. Also be sure to ask every friendly bird of the forest to be present, for we must insist upon preserving our liberty, or else be forever slaves to these rooks."

With these words he rose into the air and sped swiftly upon his errand.

The other birds looked after him earnestly.

"I think it will be well for us to follow his advice," said Judge Bullfinch, after a pause. "The bluejay is an able bird, and has had much experience. Besides, we have ever found him just and honorable since the time we made him our policeman, so I feel that we may depend upon him in this emergency."

"Why, it is all we can do," replied a robin; and this remark was so true that the birds quietly dispersed and returned to their nests to await the important meeting the next morning.

Chapter 20

The Battle

T winkle and Chubbins flew slowly home to their nests in the maple tree, pausing to ask every bird they met where tingle-berries grew. But none of them could tell.

"I'm sorry we did not ask Policeman Bluejay," said Chubbins.

"I intended to ask him, but we hadn't time," replied Twinkle. "But he will be back to-morrow morning."

"I wonder what he's going to do," remarked the boy.

"Don't know, Chub; but it'll be the right thing, whatever it is. You may be sure of that."

They visited the nest of the baby goldfinches, and found the Widow Chaffinch still caring for the orphans in her motherly way. The little ones seemed to be as hungry as ever, but the widow assured the lark-children that all five had just been fed.

"Did you ever hear of a tingle-berry?" asked Twinkle.

"Yes; it seems to me I have heard of that berry," was the reply. "If I remember rightly my grandmother once told me of the tingle-berries, and warned me never to eat one. But I am quite certain the things do not grow in our forest, for I have never seen one that I can recollect."

"Where do they grow, then?" enquired Chubbins.

"I can't say exactly where; but if they are not in the forest, they must grow in the open country."

The child-larks now returned to their own nest, and sat snug-

259

gled up in it during the evening, talking over the day's experiences and the wonderful things they had seen in the fairy-like Paradise of the Birds. So much sight-seeing had made them tired, so when it grew dark they fell fast asleep, and did not waken until the sun was peeping over the edge of the trees.

"Good gracious!" exclaimed the girl, "we shall be late at the meeting at the Judgment Tree. Let's hurry, Chub."

They ate a hasty breakfast from the contents of their basket, and after flying to the brook for a drink and a dip in the cool water they hurried toward the Judgment Tree.

There they found a fast assemblage of birds. They were so numerous, indeed, that Twinkle was surprised to find that so many of them inhabited the forest.

But a still greater surprise was in store for her, for immediately she discovered sitting upon the biggest branch of the tree twenty-two bluejays, all in a row. They were large, splendidly plumaged birds, with keen eyes and sharp bills, and at their head was the children's old friend, the policeman.

"These are my cousins," he said to the child-larks, proudly, "and I have brought them from another forest, where they live, to assist me. I am not afraid of the foolish rooks now, and in a moment we shall fly away to give them battle."

The forest birds were all in a flutter of delight at the prompt arrival of the powerful bluejays, and when the word of command was given they all left the tree and flew swiftly to meet the rooks.

First came the ranks of the twenty-two bluejays, with the policeman at their head. Then followed many magpies and cuckoos, who were too clever to side with the naughty rooks when they saw the powerful birds the bluejay had summoned to his assistance. After these flew the smaller birds, of all descriptions, and they were so many and at the same time so angry that they were likely to prove stubborn foes in a fight.

This vast army came upon the rooks in an open space in the forest. Without waiting for any words or explanations from the rebels, the soldierly bluejays fell upon their enemies instantly, fighting fiercely with bill and claw, while the other birds fluttered in the rear, awaiting their time to join in the affray.

Policeman Bluejay singled out the rook which had stolen his helmet and club, and dashed upon him so furiously that the black rebel was amazed, and proved an easy victim to the other's superior powers. He threw down the club and helmet at once; but the bluejay was not satisfied with that, and attacked the thief again and again, until the air was full of black feathers torn from the rook's body.

After all, the battle did not last long; for the rooks soon screamed for mercy, and found themselves badly plucked and torn by the time their assailants finally decided they had been punished enough.

Like all blustering, evil-disposed people, when they found themselves conquered they whined and humbled themselves before the victors and declared they would never again rebel against Policeman Bluejay, the regularly appointed guardian of the Law of the Forest. And I am told that after this day the rooks, who are not rightly forest birds, betook themselves to the nearest villages and farm houses, and contented themselves with plaguing mankind, who could not revenge themselves as easily as the birds did.

After the fight Policeman Bluejay thanked his cousins and sent them home again, and then the birds all surrounded the policeman and cheered him gratefully for his cleverness and bravery, so that he was the hero of the hour.

Judge Bullfinch tried to make a fine speech, but the birds

were too excited to listen to his words, and he soon found himself without an audience.

Of course, Twinkle and Chubbins took no part in the fight, but they had hovered in the background to watch it, and were therefore as proud of their friend as any of the forest birds could be.

Chapter 21

The Tingle-Berries

When the excitement of the morning had subsided and the forest was quiet again, Policeman Bluejay came to the nest of the child-larks, wearing his official helmet and club. You may be sure that one of the first things Twinkle asked him was if he knew where tingle-berries grew.

"Of course," he replied, promptly. "They grow over at the north edge of the forest, in the open country. But you must never eat them, my dear friend, because they are very bad for birds."

"But the Royal Necromancer of the King Bird of Paradise says the tingle-berries will restore us to our proper forms," explained the girl.

"Oh; did he say that? Then he probably knows," said the bluejay, "and I will help you to find the berries. We birds always avoid them, for they give us severe pains in our stomachs."

"That's bad," observed Chubbins, uneasily.

"Well," said Twinkle, "I'd be willing to have a pain or two, just to be myself again."

"So would I, if it comes to that," agreed the boy. "But I'd rather have found a way to be myself without getting the pain."

"There is usually but one thing that will overcome an enchantment," remarked the bluejay, seriously; "and if it is a tingle-berry that will destroy the charm which the old tuxix

263

put upon you, then nothing else will answer the same purpose. The Royal Necromancer is very wise, and you may depend upon what he says. But it is late, at this season, for tingle-berries. They do not grow at all times of the year, and we may not be able to find any upon the bushes."

"Cannot we go at once and find out?" asked Twinkle, anxiously.

"To be sure. It will grieve me to lose you, my little friends, but I want to do what will give you the most happiness. Come with me, please."

They flew away through the forest, and by and by came upon the open country to the north, leaving all the trees behind them.

"Why, this is the place we entered the forest, that day we got 'chanted!" cried Twinkle.

"So it is," said Chubbins. "I believe we could find our way home from here, Twink."

"But we can't go home like we are," replied the girl-lark. "What would our folks say, to find us with birds' bodies?"

"They'd yell and run," declared the boy.

"Then," said she, "we must find the tingle-berries."

The bluejay flew with them to some bushes which he said were the kind the tingle-berries grew upon, but they were all bare and not a single berry could be found.

"There must be more not far away," said the policeman, encouragingly. "Let us look about us."

They found several clumps of the bushes, to be sure; but unfortunately no berries were now growing upon them, and at each failure the children grew more and more sad and despondent.

"If we have to wait until the bushes bear again," Twinkle remarked, "it will be nearly a year, and I'm sure we can't live in the forest all winter."

"Why not?" asked the policeman.

"The food in our basket would all be gone, and then we would starve to death," was the reply. "We can't eat bugs and worms, you know."

"I'd rather die!" declared Chubbins, mournfully.

The bluejay became very thoughtful.

"If we could find some of the tingle bushes growing near the shade of the forest," he said at last, "there might still be some berries remaining on them. Out here in the bright sunshine the berries soon wither and drop off and disappear."

"Then let us look near the trees," suggested Twinkle.

They searched for a long time unsuccessfully. It was growing late, and they were almost in despair, when a sharp cry from Policeman Bluejay drew the child-larks to his side.

"What is it?" enquired the girl, trembling with nervous excitement.

"Why," said the policeman, "here is a bush at last, and on it are exactly two ripe tingle-berries!"

Chapter 22

The Transformation

They looked earnestly at the bush, and saw that their friend spoke truly. Upon a high limb was one plump, red berry, looking much like a cranberry, while lower down grew another but smaller berry, which appeared to be partially withered.

"Good!" the lark-children cried, joyfully; and the next moment Chubbins added: "You eat the big berry, Twink."

"Why?" she asked, hesitating.

"It looks as if it had more stomach-ache in it," he replied.

"I'm not afraid of that," said she. "But do you suppose the little berry will be enough for you? One side of it is withered, you see.

"That won't matter," returned the boy-lark. "The Royal Necromancer said to eat one berry. He didn't say a little or a big one, you know, or whether it should be plump or withered."

"That is true," said the girl-lark. "Shall I eat mine now?"

"The sooner the better," Chubbins replied.

"Don't forget me, little friend, when you are a human again," said Policeman Bluejay, sadly.

"I shall never forget you," Twinkle answered, "nor any part of all your kindness to us. We shall be friends forever."

That seemed to please the handsome blue bird, and Twinkle

was so eager that she could not wait to say more. She plucked the big, plump berry, put it in her mouth with her little claw, and ate it as soon as possible.

In a moment she said: "Ouch! Oo-oo-oo!" But it did not hurt so badly, after all. Her form quickly changed and grew larger; and while Chubbins and Policeman Bluejay watched her anxiously she became a girl again, and the bird's body with its soft gray feathers completely disappeared.

A she felt herself changing she called: "Good-bye!" to the bluejay; but even then he could hardly understand her words.

"Good-bye!" he answered, and to Twinkle's ears it sounded like "Chir-r-rip-chee-wee!"

"How did it feel? asked Chubbins; but she looked at him queerly, as if his language was strange to her, and seemed to be half frightened.

"Guess I'll have to eat my berry," he said, with a laugh, and proceeded to pluck and eat it, as Twinkle had done. He yelled once or twice at the cramp the fruit gave him, but as soon as the pain ceased he began to grow and change in the same way his little comrade had.

But not entirely. For although he got his human body and legs back again, all in their natural sizes, his wings remained as they were, and it startled him to find that the magic power had passed and he was still partly a bird.

"What's the matter?" asked Twinkle.

"Is anything wrong?" enquired the bluejay.

The boy understood them both, although they could not now understand each other. He said to Twinkle:

"I guess the berry wasn't quite big enough." Then he repeated the same thing in the bird language to Policeman Bluejay, and it sounded to Twinkle like:

"Pir-r-r-r — eep — cheep — tweet!"

"What in the world can you do?" asked the girl, quite distressed. "It will be just dreadful if you have to stay like that."

The tears came to Chubbins' eyes. He tried to restrain them, but could not. He flapped his little wings dolefully and said:

"I wish I was either one thing or the other! I'd rather be a child-lark again, and nest in a tree, than to go home to the folks in this way."

Policeman Bluejay had seen his dilemma at the first, and his sharp eyes had been roving over all the bushes that were within the range of his vision. Suddenly he uttered a chirp of delight and dashed away, speedily returning with another tingle-berry in his bill.

"It's the very last one there is!" said he to Chubbins.

"But it is all that I want," cried the boy, brightening at once; and then, regardless of any pain, he ate the berry as greedily as if he was fond of a stomach-ache.

The second berry had a good effect in one way, for Chubbins' wings quickly became arms, and he was now as perfectly formed as he had been before he met with the cruel tuxix. But he gave a groan, every once in a while, and Twinkle suspected that two berries were twice as powerful as one, and made a pain that lasted twice as long.

As the boy and girl looked around they were astonished to find their basket standing on the ground beside them. On a limb of the first tree of the forest sat silently regarding them a big blue bird that they knew must be Policeman Bluejay, although somehow or other he had lost his glossy black helmet and the club he had carried underneath his wing.

"It's almost dark," said Twinkle, yawning. "Let's go home, Chub."

"All right."

"It's almost dark. Let's go home."

He picked up the basket, and for a few minutes they walked along in silence.

Then the boy asked:

"Don't your legs feel heavy, Twink?"

"Yes," said she; "do yours?"

"Awful," said he.